NAOMI'S STORY

A Hollybrook Amish Romance

BRENDA MAXFIELD

Hollybrook Amish Romance

Table of Contents

BYLER'S BED & BREAKFAST

Chapter One

*The thief cometh not, but for to steal, and to kill, and to destroy: I am come that
they might have life, and that they might have it more abundantly.*
John 10:10 (King James Version)

Naomi Byler stared at the ledger book, praying the numbers would
magically morph into something with promise. Maybe if she squeezed
her hazel eyes closed and then fluttered them open again, the minus
sign would become a plus, and all would be well. But she knew it was
hopeless. She blinked twice. It was no use.

She worked to keep her thin shoulders from slumping. She spent too
much of each day curled in on herself, shielding her heart. As if that
would help.

"Mama!" Katy cried as she rushed into the front room where Naomi
sat at the heavy oak desk. "Ben's awake."

Naomi gazed at her eleven-year-old daughter. Katy stood before her,
panting slightly. As usual, strands of auburn hair had escaped her *kapp*
and wisped about her face as if she were standing in a continual breeze.
Her large blue eyes, looking as if they held a thousand mysteries, stared
back at her mother.

"Is he up, then?" Naomi asked.

"*Nee*. He's rustling about, though, and should be down in a minute. Should I pour the milk?"

"*Jah*. I'll be right in."

Katy ran off to the kitchen, and Naomi rose from the desk. Looking at the books so early in the morning did her no favors. The mood was now set for the day. She knew it wasn't wise to sit and figure the numbers over and over, but they plagued her mind in the wee hours of the night, and nearly every morning saw her sitting at the desk her brother-in-law had made for her husband, Isaac. Her *dead* husband, Isaac. Naomi sucked in air and hesitated before joining her daughter. She couldn't let Katy see her again with tears in her eyes. The poor child had witnessed her mother crying too many times of late.

She squared her shoulders and walked with determination into the kitchen. Katy had lit the lamp in the early morning darkness and was busy pouring the milk. "Mama, didn't you make the eggs yet?"

Why, of course, she had. Naomi glanced at the stove. It sat there, pristinely clean, with nary a skillet in sight. She swallowed hard and realized that once again, she'd neglected her basic duties. Not only neglected them, but didn't even remember that she hadn't done them. What was happening to her? Did Isaac take her mind with him when he passed?

"I thought we could make the eggs together," Naomi said, as if that had been her plan all along.

Katy gave her mother a questioning look but then smiled. "I like cooking eggs with you."

Bless you, child. Naomi knew her daughter was wiser than her years, and thanked God for her. Katy took the bowl of eggs from the fridge and carried them to the counter. "I'll collect today's eggs later this morning, Mama. Don't you worry."

Naomi gave her a grateful smile. "I'm not worried, Katy girl." A flash of guilt swept through her. More and more often, Naomi felt their roles were reversed and Katy had become the adult, and Naomi had become the child. It wasn't good. Or right. But Naomi hardly had the energy to turn it around.

Lately, she hadn't the energy for much of anything. Except worry. Somehow, she always managed to have energy for that.

"Morning, Mama," Ben said from the doorway. His sandy blond hair was tussled, and he had sleep in his eyes. Naomi opened her arms to him, and he ran to her, squeezing her around the waist.

"Did you sleep well, little man?"

Ben nodded and let her go. "I'm hungry."

"We're cooking eggs," Katy said, breaking the last two into the skillet. A pleasant sizzle filled the air. "I'm gonna fry them this time." She held the spatula up like a banner. "Mama, I'm not gonna break any of the yolks. You just watch and see."

"That's my girl," Naomi said. She gave a small chuckle. "Katy, you're going to fly right past me as the cook of the house."

Katy grinned, a happy flush covering her cheeks. "Ah, Mama. I could never cook as good as you."

In truth, Naomi was an excellent cook. Isaac used to brag about the fluffiness of her biscuits and the flakiness of her pie crusts. And then he would kiss her cheek—right in front of the children. Naomi loved it. She loved *him*. She had often wondered if Isaac was a particularly affectionate man because both his parents died when he was young. He was raised by his eldest brother back in Pennsylvania; in effect, becoming one of his brother's brood. So Isaac knew the brevity of life and had relished every moment.

The familiar tightness in her chest made it difficult to breathe. She looked away, pretending to need something in a far cupboard.

"Take the glasses to the table, Ben. Okay?" Katy directed.

Ben obediently took two glasses of milk to the table. In a moment, he was back for the third.

"I did it!" Katy cried, brandishing the spatula. "Look, Mama! No broken yolks!"

Naomi moved to the stove and inspected the eggs. "No broken yolks," she repeated. "Good job."

No broken yolks. But plenty *was* broken in the Byler household—ever since the accident that had snatched the lives of her husband and her parents from the earth. Naomi watched her two children fussing over the plates and eggs and thanked God for the thousandth time that she hadn't let them climb into the van that late winter morning.

Her mind traveled back to the fateful day, as it often did. She wished she could forget it. Forget it all. But every detail was branded into her heart and her mind, and she couldn't shake them nor stop them from playing over and over and over again.

"Come on, Naomi. The kids will like the outing," Isaac had urged her.

It wasn't often she had countered Isaac's wishes, but that morning she was sewing outfits for both children, and she'd wanted them there to try the pieces on. She didn't want to wait till late afternoon when they would return.

"And the kids will enjoy seeing the Grayson's llamas," Isaac had continued.

Which was true. Especially Ben. That child loved everything that breathed. But for some reason, Naomi had held firm. "They can go with you next time," she'd said. "I know *Dat* will be going back soon to pick up more seed."

Her *dat* had only recently bought the farm they all lived on, bringing them to Hollybrook, Indiana, and a new district of Amish folk. He'd been toying with the idea of leasing land in Pennsylvania where they had lived, but when this land came up for sale, he'd jumped at the chance. He had taken out a mortgage, something Amish were averse to doing. But buying land, farming equipment, and perhaps even a carriage, were considered acceptable reasons to carry a debt. And paying it off in a timely manner was considered a moral obligation.

And so her *dat* had taken out the loan with the intent to pay it back well before it went full term. To that end, he was determined to grow the best, heartiest crops of wheat in the community. He had it in mind to collect special summer seed from the Graysons who lived upstate. Mr. Grayson claimed his seed produced a harvest fifty percent richer and more prolific than regular seed. Thing was, the local Feed & Supply wouldn't carry it. So *Dat*, *Mamm*, and Isaac had hired a Mennonite driver to take them north to pick it up personally.

It was silly, really. Three people to collect seed. But the winter had been long, and they had all felt the effects of cabin fever. So, the trip was planned for them all. But Naomi had been stubborn.

Even now, she wondered whether it was God who had kept her and the children from taking that trip. She shuddered, and her hand went to her throat. It made no sense. If God could keep her and the children from going, why hadn't He kept them *all* from going?

When her parents and husband hadn't arrived back that evening, Naomi let the children stay up late to wait for them. *Dat* always held the evening Bible reading and prayer, and it didn't feel right to go to bed without him leading it.

Naomi had been in the kitchen fussing with a special treat of hot chocolate when she heard Katy's voice.

"Mama! Look at the lights!"

Then Ben had chimed in. "Police!" he cried with excitement. "Mama! The police are visiting us."

Naomi's heart had lurched to her throat, and she went running to the front room. She pushed the children behind her and flung open the door. Two state patrolmen had gotten out of the flashing car and were climbing the steps of the porch. Naomi watched them move closer as if in slow motion. One of them raised his foot and placed it on the first step. Then he gave his partner a solemn glance. His partner frowned and mounted the step behind him. While Naomi's breath froze in her throat, they came nearer and nearer and grew larger and larger.

She stared at them through a veil of tears which hovered on her thick lashes, refusing to fall. Katy peered out from behind her and then stepped to her side. Ben stayed put. Naomi felt him grip the back of her dress in his fist.

"Ma'am," the first officer said. His voice was rich and low and heavy with regret. "Are you Mrs. Byler? Mrs. Naomi Byler?"

She nodded, surprised her joints worked and that she could move at all.

"Would the children like to wait for you inside?" the other officer asked. He smiled at Katy and craned his head a bit, as if trying to get a look at Ben.

Naomi worked to swallow. Her throat had gone bone dry. She blinked like a child who had spied a monster lurking in the shadows. "*Nee,*" she managed to eke out. "They can hear what you have to say."

The second officer shuffled his foot over the well-worn porch step. He coughed and glanced at his buddy.

"Well, then," the first officer said. "We're very sorry to inform you that there's been an accident."

Katy grabbed Naomi's hand tight. Naomi winced, not taking her eyes from the officer.

"Your parents and your husband..." Here he paused as if he was having trouble bringing himself to say the words. "I'm sorry." Another pause. "They did not survive the crash."

Naomi's knees buckled, and the officer reached out, grabbing her before she fell to the porch. The world swam before Naomi's eyes, and she heard Katy cry out. Ben burst into tears.

"Get her inside," said the second man. "Take her inside."

Together, the two of them half carried her into the front room where they set her on the davenport. Katy leaned close, her eyes round and full of tears. "Mama, what do they mean? Are they dead?"

Ben stood in the middle of the room, wailing.

The first officer squatted before Naomi. "Ma'am, can we get you anything? Is there anyone to call?"

The second officer swatted his shoulder and gave him a look. The first officer's face turned red as he must have realized there would be no phones.

A sharp agonizing pain seared through Naomi's heart. *Dead? All* three *of them?* "What happened?" she uttered, reaching toward Ben. Ben ran into her arms and fell against her shoulder. Katy collapsed next to her on the couch.

"A mini-bus ran a stop sign. It was going too fast, well over the speed limit. It barreled right into the van."

"And our driver?"

"In the hospital. I'm not sure if he'll pull through."

Naomi's head fell back against the couch. Her mind scrambled, trying to make sense of it.

"I want my *dat!*" Katy sniveled. "Mama, where is he?"

Naomi put her arm around Katy's shoulders, and the girl slumped into Ben against Naomi's chest.

"Where are they?" Naomi asked.

"At the coroner's. In town."

Naomi nodded, and for a split second she thought she would vomit. She swallowed again, hard, forcing the bile back down her throat.

"Is there anything we can do for you?" the second officer asked. "Anything? Anything at all?"

She shook her head as a thick fog settled over her.

Isaac. Isaac. Isaac. A sharp pain came alive, tearing through her lungs. The fog swirled about her head and disappeared, leaving everything in sharp focus.

"Thank you," she said, her voice brittle. She stood, and the children fell together behind her. "I'll see you to the door."

"Oh, ma'am, that's not necessary," the first man said.

She moved to the door as if her limbs were connected by moving screws. She opened the door, and both men retreated down the steps. The second officer paused at the bottom step and looked back up at her, his wide-set brown eyes full of sorrow.

That next week, after the nightmare of funerals and mountains of casseroles and weeping friends passed, she and the children had moved from the *daadi haus* into the big house. And it wasn't long before she forced herself to open the ledger books and try to make sense of what she saw. She had always been good at figures, but her eighth grade education hadn't prepared her for what she now faced. She had no knowledge of how mortgage interest worked, nor where to go to learn.

All she did know was that she needed a great sum of money every month to keep afloat. A great sum of money she did not have. Since then, every month saw the burden that pressed on her shoulders get larger and grow more wieldy.

She shuddered. Enough. *Enough*.

"Take the plates in, Katy," she directed her daughter.

Katy had already dished up the eggs and set a thick slice of bread on each plate. She gladly did her mother's bidding and took the breakfast in to the dining table. Ben was already seated, rubbing at his eyes.

"I need you children to muck out the barn this morning," Naomi instructed. "And perhaps in the afternoon, we can have a bit of a picnic on the front porch."

Katy's eyes went round, and she stared at her mother. "Really? We can have dinner outside?"

Naomi nearly wept at the look of excitement on her daughter's face. "*Jah*. Why not?"

Ben grinned. "A picnic." He shook his head and reached for the bread on his plate.

"Benjamin!" Naomi scolded. "Let us give the silent blessing first, *jah?*"

Dutifully, Ben folded his hands. The three of them bowed their heads. Naomi worked to keep her mind off her worries and focus on God. She thanked Him for the health of her children and the sunny weather and... She tried to go further, but her mind flapped back to the ledger books. She sighed and gave a small cough, signaling the end of the prayer.

The three of them tucked into the food, Katy jabbering about her friend Liz next door, who had named every one of their fourteen hens.

Chapter Two

Naomi stood over the counter, dots of wayward flour up her arms. She pressed her hands into the bread dough, knotting and pulling and smoothing and plumping. She'd been kneading it for nearly twenty minutes, much longer than necessary. She'd probably have a loaf of rubber when it was baked. She sighed. That's what you got when your mind wasn't on the work at hand.

She gazed out the kitchen window and saw Zachariah King approach the house. His dark blue shirt hung a bit rumpled off his broad shoulders, and the left side was coming untucked, barely held in place by a black suspender. He wore a straw hat, which he removed as he drew close to the steps. He came around to the front door as if he were a proper guest, instead of the young farmer who was leasing her land. She'd told him time and again that he could come to the side door, but he always refused with an embarrassed look and his eyes cast to the ground.

Naomi blew out her breath and ran her hands over the edge of her *kapp*, ensuring that every hair was tucked securely in place. Then she smoothed down her dress, eliminating any wrinkles. Truth was that even when feeling her worst, Naomi Byler looked tidy and in control.

Too bad I don't feel in control.

Isaac used to call her beautiful. She would feign dismay, knowing that personal vanity was to be avoided at all costs. But secretly, in her heart of hearts, Isaac's loving compliments made her feel warm and secure and special. She grimaced. Life had now taught her only too well what vanity could bring. She shuddered. Did she really believe her moments of vanity had brought about her tragedy of loss? Did she really believe that's how life worked?

There was a gentle rap on the front door. She walked to it, opened it wide, and gazed up at Zachariah.

His hat was off, and he fingered the wide brim, circling the diameter again and again with this calloused hands. "I wanted to let you know that I'll get your payment to you by the end of the week."

"I'm not worried," she said, a kind smile on her face. "I know you'll pay me."

How she wished she could count on other things the way she could count on Zachariah's payments. Shortly after the tragic accident, he'd come to her and asked if he could farm her family's land. At first, she was hesitant. It seemed disloyal to allow someone else to work the land her father and husband had been so keen to farm. But after she realized the seriousness of her situation, she had agreed. And so far, it was working well. But she knew the summer and harvest season wouldn't last forever, and then his payments would stop—until the next planting season. *Hopefully.*

"Zachariah?"

He glanced at her, and she noticed how starkly blue his eyes were. They reminded her of the deep color on the border of Ida Mae's favorite quilt—true and bright and pleasant.

"Jah?"

"I know it's early and all," she said, and her voice carried the barest hint of a quiver, "but I was wondering if you'd be needing my fields next spring, too."

Zachariah slapped his hat against his thigh, shaking loose the dust of the fields, and paused, as if pondering her question. Then he looked at her, and she felt the power behind his gaze. "Would it be helpful if I was?"

She hesitated, suddenly feeling exposed and uncomfortable. His gaze often did that to her, and she wasn't sure why. Only that when he looked at her, it was as if they were all alone in the world. Everything else faded into the background. "I was just wondering, that's all," she continued. She took a step back, feeling foolish.

"*Jah*," he said quickly, his eyes still steady on hers. He leaned forward. "I will likely be needing your land next year, too."

A wave of relief blotted out her discomfort. *He needs the land.* She'd have that income for those months at least.

"Naomi, I'll be paying you for the use of your land all year." His brows drew into a frown. "Didn't you understand that? It's how it works. A person doesn't just lease the use of the land for a few months. It's an around-the-year arrangement."

Her lips parted in surprise. "Doesn't seem quite fair to me. You aren't using it during the winter."

"Did your husband and *dat* farm back in Pennsylvania?"

"They raised goats mostly. Sold both the goats and the milk. But my *dat* farmed as a lad. He was eager to get back to it." Her voice caught, and she felt her cheeks go hot.

"It's a year-round job. Trust me on that."

"But—"

"Count on my payment all year," he said gruffly. He paused for a moment, before pressing his hat back on his head. He smiled then, and she was startled at the glow of interest in his eyes.

He turned to leave, and she watched him go, surprised at her sudden urge to call out his name. But what for? She had nothing more to say. Nor did he. Why then, would she want him to come back? It made no sense, but a strange feeling of loss filled her as his figure grew more distant. She leaned against the doorframe and observed his easy saunter across her drive, down to the barn, and on to the fields. *Zachariah King.* He was a good man. A bit quiet, maybe, but good.

The clip clop of a horse interrupted her reverie, and she saw Mary Mullen approach in her pony cart. She held the reins loosely, and her bun looked a bit scraggly beneath her *kapp*. Naomi grinned. Mary always looked as if she had just scrambled barefoot through a field chasing a runaway hen.

"Naomi!" she hollered in her cheery voice. "Naomi! I have a job for you!"

Naomi walked down the steps to greet her. "Hello, Mary. What brings you by?"

Mary shifted her pudgy body on the cart's bench, facing Naomi squarely. "How do you feel about whipping up a dozen pies this afternoon?"

"A dozen? Why?" Naomi was already ticking through the ingredients she could use to make that many pies so quickly.

"I've fallen behind. You know my Jeremy had a fever yesterday, and I spent hours running back and forth with cold cloths and tea. That child done wore me to a frazzle. And now Lucas is sniffling something fierce. If the girls get it, I'm done for."

"*Ach.* I'm sorry. So you need the pies for your roadside stand?"

"That I do. And you'd keep the money, of course. You do realize that a good homemade Amish pie can bring you fifteen dollars and more?"

Naomi blinked. She knew Mary had run a roadside stand during the summer for the last few years. But, being new to Hollybrook, she didn't know much about her friend's business. More than fifteen dollars a pie? She could make some serious money.

"I'll do it," she said quickly. "What time do you need them?"

Mary scratched her head, displacing her *kapp* by a few inches. "I get a surge of traffic in the late afternoon and early evening. And the pies will keep well for tomorrow if I don't sell them all today. Sorry to give you so little notice."

Naomi shook her head. "No worries. It will be a help to me, too."

"All right then. Can you deliver them by five?"

Naomi calculated the time. It would be close. "I'll do my best."

"*Gut*. See you then." Mary swatted her pony with the reins and before she was out of sight, Naomi was already running out back around the house.

"Katy!" she called. "Katy! Come quick. I need you!"

She hurried back into the kitchen to put a cloth over her bread dough. It could rise while she got busy on the crusts. Katy came bursting into the kitchen.

"What is it, Mama?"

"We're going to make a dozen pies. Get the tins out of the cupboard." Naomi flew about the kitchen, pulling out a can of lard. She heaved her twenty-five pound bag of flour in from the pantry. "Call your brother. We're all going to need to help on this!"

Katy spread the pie tins across the counter and then flew outside hollering for her brother. Naomi dragged a bushel of apples from the corner, and turning on the faucet, she ran handfuls of them beneath the water. How she wished she had the peeler she'd seen in the Groyer's kitchen back in Pennsylvania. She'd never beheld such a wonder. You fastened the apple into the contraption and turned a crank, and after mere moments, there it was: a peeled apple. Well, she'd have to do it the old-fashioned way with a paring knife.

She could set Katy to making some lemon pudding, though. And Ben could help fetch whatever was needed.

Ben came tumbling into the kitchen after Katy. "We're making pies?" he asked, with a silly grin. "I been wanting some pie."

"Not for you, Ben. We're going to sell these pies and make some money." Naomi was actually excited about the prospect, knowing she was doing something constructive to earn their keep.

"Can't I have a piece?" Ben whined.

Naomi laughed. "We'll see. Maybe we can make one extra."

Katy giggled. "Sounds like a fine idea to me."

Naomi was already sifting flour into a large glass bowl. "Ben, grab me that wooden spoon, would you?" She nodded toward the counter. "And get the salt."

The kitchen became a dusty flurry as the three of them hustled about, measuring, cutting, peeling, and rolling. Halfway through, Naomi glanced up at the kitchen clock. "Faster, children! We're not going to make our deadline."

"*Mamm*, there aren't enough apples for this one," Katy said, a stripe of flour across her cheek. "And we're out."

"Put in a pear," Ben suggested.

"We don't have any pears!"

"How about a peach?" he suggested.

"We don't have peaches, either."

Naomi's gaze flew about the kitchen. She spotted a quart jar of apple marmalade on the shelf. "We can use the marmalade," she said. "Will it be enough?"

Katy ran to get it, twisted off the ring and then flipped off the lid with the edge of a butter knife. She was about to stick her finger into the rich jam-like substance when Naomi stopped her.

"Don't you go sticking your finger in there, Katy Byler! We can't be selling your germs at the roadside stand, now can we?"

Katy gave a sheepish giggle and scooped the marmalade over the apple filling already in the crust. She spread it around evenly and then stood back with a look of admiration on her young face. "What do you think, *Mamm*?"

"I think it's going to be the best pie we bake today. Ben, help Katy put on the top crust."

They were back at it, the heat from the cooking stove filling the kitchen until all three of them had red faces wet with perspiration. When the last two pies were put in the oven, they all three collapsed onto the kitchen bench.

"We done it," Ben said. "Can I have my piece now?"

Naomi reached over and tousled his hair, making it stand up in spikes. "We made a dozen, and we're out of ingredients." But she rushed on. "I tell you what. I'll sprinkle the extra scraps of dough with sugar and cinnamon and bake them for you to munch on. How's that?"

Ben grinned. "Okay." He jumped up. "Let's do it now."

Naomi shook her head in amusement and got up to grab a cookie sheet. She spread the scraps of dough over the surface and sprinkled them with the sweet mixture.

"Soon as the last pie comes out, we'll stick these in. You can eat them on the way to the stand. Now, both of you go wash up a bit. You look like you've been inside a bakery that exploded."

They went to the washroom near the side entrance. She heard them jabbering about the pie crusts and all the work they'd done. She was proud of them. Ever since ... well ... ever since the accident, they'd pulled together to help her in so many ways. Katy, especially. The child was grown-up well beyond her eleven years.

Naomi grabbed up the dirty cooking utensils and dropped them into the sink. She'd like to do something especially nice for Katy one of these days. In gratitude. She began washing the dishes when she remembered the rising bread.

"*Ach!* The bread!" she cried, running into the panty. The dough had risen and slopped over the side of the bowl in a spongy mess, taking with it the dishtowel she'd draped over the top hours earlier. She stared at the disaster as if it had somehow betrayed her. Then realizing how silly she was being and that the whole thing was her fault, she gathered up the entire jumble and carried it outside to dump into the garbage bin.

She knew it was going to take a bit of washing to get that dishtowel clean again.

~

Ben and Katy had hitched up Molly to the pony cart, and Katy had expertly driven the cart up to the front porch.

"We're ready, Mama!" she called in through the door.

"I've got the pies boxed up. Come help me carry!" Naomi called back.

The children dashed inside, and Naomi slowed them to a crawl after she gave them each a box containing two pies. "We'll set these in the back of the cart and then come back for the rest," she directed.

All the boxes fit quite tidily into the bed of the cart. Naomi spread a clean sheet over the top of all the boxes and then climbed into the driver's spot. "All aboard!" she said with a grin. "Now, let's go sell some pies."

The drive to Mary's roadside stand didn't take long. When they pulled into the parking area at the side of the road, Katy was delighted to holler a greeting when she saw her friend Liz hanging about. As soon as Katy helped Naomi unload the boxes, she was off with Liz, chatting and laughing. Ben hung around the tables laden with baked goods and a stunning display of tomatoes, squash, green beans, beets, and other freshly plucked vegetables.

"Your pies are lovely," Mary said, panting a bit as she moved some of the piles of vegetables about to make extra room. "I knew they would be."

"How are your boys? Any better?" Naomi asked.

"I should hope so. I'm worn down to a stick caring for them." Mary gave a hearty chuckle.

Naomi joined in the laughter, feeling more chipper than she had in weeks. If she could sell all twelve of her pies, she would have nearly two hundred dollars by the end of the day. If that was the kind of profit she could be looking at, perhaps she should start a roadside stand of her own. But as soon as she thought of the idea, she dismissed it. How could she encroach on Mary's territory? It wouldn't be seemly at all.

"Do you want to go and check on them?" Naomi asked. "I can watch the stand for you."

Mary glanced over her shoulder to where her farmhouse sat, not so far away. "I've put Betty in charge, but I declare that girl would lose her head given half a minute."

Naomi chuckled. "Go on with you, then. You'll rest easier knowing everything's all right."

Mary gave Naomi's arm a squeeze. "You're right at that. Cash box is over yonder." She nodded her head to a small table at the back of the stand. "Prices are clear. You can price your pies as you see fit."

"Thank you, Mary."

Mary nodded and rushed off toward her house. Ben plopped himself down on one of the available chairs and promptly looked bored.

Katy wandered into the stand, Liz at her heels. "*Mamm*, can I run to Liz's house? Did you know there's a big toad living in one of their trees?"

"Is that right?" Naomi asked. "Well, then, I guess you better hustle on over there to see it."

"A toad?" Ben perked up. "I wanna see it!"

Katy gave her mother a forlorn look. "Does he have to?"

"Katy Byler, of course, he has to. You mind him well and be back here before dark."

"That's forever!" Ben cried, jumping from his chair. "It don't get dark till we're in bed."

Katy rolled her eyes and looped her arm through Liz's. "You better not talk our ears off," she warned Ben, looking at him over her shoulder. "And I mean it."

Katy and Liz took off at a quick pace with Ben scrambling to catch up. Naomi's heart followed her children as they left. They were doing much better than before. Especially Ben. During those first weeks after the accident, the boy would hardly speak at all. He moved around the house like an empty shell, black smudges beneath his eyes. Naomi had feared for his health, pleading to God both day and night. And slowly, slowly, he'd come out of it. Now, he was almost normal again.

Normal? Would any of them ever be *normal* again?

Chapter Three

A white car pulled up, spitting gravel and dust. A man, looking to be in his early thirties, climbed out. He was tall and his chin was covered with the stubble of a few days of missed shaves. He wore sunglasses, and his dark hair hung casually over his forehead, skimming the tops of his ears. He had on jeans and a button-down shirt, tucked in. Naomi noted that he also wore cowboy boots.

"Hello, ma'am," he said to Naomi n a rich drawl. He took off his sunglasses, revealing extraordinary brown eyes, flecked and ringed with gold.

Naomi faced him, feeling the energy of his presence.

"I'm wondering where a guy might find a place to stay for a few days." He hung his sunglasses on the front of his shirt collar, and then he stretched and rolled his head as if he'd been sitting for much too long. Naomi was transfixed by his very size—his height, his wide set of shoulders, the way his long torso looked in his rumpled shirt.

For a moment, she didn't answer, but when she saw his intent gaze on her, she realized he needed an answer.

"There's a hotel in town. Two, actually, I think."

"You're right about that," he said with a slow smile. "Thing is, they're both full up. I guess lots of folks came in for the county fair."

She gave a start. She'd forgotten about the fair; although, how she could have was beyond her. Plenty of the people in her district entered quilts and jams and jellies and other canned goods to be judged. Cash prizes were given, too. Truth be told, her Amish friends usually won everything.

Or so she was told, not having been in the area to attend one herself.

Again, she realized the *Englischer* was staring at her, and her face grew warm. "If they're full up, you might try traveling to Linder's Corner. It's not too far."

He stepped closer, and she caught the faint smell of some kind of pine cologne. "I was hoping to stay right in Hollybrook," he said. "I'm a journalist, you see. I'm covering the fair for the magazine I write for. *Across America*, it's called. Have you read it?"

She shook her head.

He laughed, and the sound was deep and warm and rich. "Didn't reckon you had. But you ought to, you know. Some mighty good writers in there!"

She couldn't help but smile.

"No, what I was hoping for was some kind of Bed and Breakfast." He gazed around and then looked back at her. "Do you know of one?"

She'd heard of Bed and Breakfast places before. In fact, the Widow Maeve Bowman ran one back in Pennsylvania, right in her previous district as a matter of fact. She had obtained special permission from the bishop to install electricity and a phone with a pledge to use them only for her business. It worked out well for her. She supported herself and her five children on it.

Her mind whirled. Why couldn't she do the same? She had the *daadi haus*. That could hold two sets of guests. And if necessary, she could fix up one of the upstairs rooms for an additional guest. Two, really. As her thoughts raced ahead, a hopeful smile tugged at her lips. She could do it. Surely, she could. Why, now that she thought of it, her house had once had electricity. It had been stripped out when they bought it. How much would it cost to reinstall?

"Ma'am?" the stranger questioned, a concerned look on his face.

"*Ach*, I'm sorry." She straightened her posture. "How much would you be spending per night?"

His brow crinkled, and he gave her a long look. "Usually I pay anywhere from ninety dollars and up for a room."

"Per night?" she asked, her eyebrows rising.

"Yes, ma'am. That's normal."

She swallowed and made a rash decision to plunge forward. "It just so happens that I take in guests."

His lips parted. "Do you, now?"

"*Jah*, I do. It will cost one hundred dollars per night. Breakfast included. In truth, you can eat all your meals with us if you choose."

"Does your husband know you take in guests?" he asked, and she saw immediately that he knew she'd never in her life taken in paying guests.

"My husband ... my husband has passed." She swallowed again, feeling the familiar lump grow in her throat. She coughed, annoyed with herself. She didn't have time to wallow in her grief now. "You'll be getting a true Amish experience," she went on. "We have no electricity."

"I'm sorry about your husband." He was quiet for a moment. Then he continued, "How about hot water?"

"Oh yes. We have a hot water heater using propane gas."

He was grinning now, a wide smile that covered his face. "Why, that sounds perfect." He gave a quick glance at his car. "My computer's battery gives me about four hours. Is there a place with electricity close by?"

She tilted her head, indicating down the road. "In town, of course."

"I'll be staying five nights," he said. "Assuming you'll have me for that long."

Naomi clasped her hands to her chest and worked to keep her excitement at bay. *Five hundred dollars.* She gave him a solemn look. "That should be fine."

"My name is Justin Moore." He extended his hand. "Nice to meet you."

She stared at his outstretched hand. Was she to touch this stranger now? This *male* stranger? Well, that's what she'd just signed up for with her impulsive decision. She reached out and shook his hand, stunned at the last five minutes of her life. "My name is Naomi Byler. My farm is just down the road. I can't leave right now as I'm watching the stand for my friend Mary."

"No problem, Ms. Byler," he said, his voice rolling over her name like a song. "If you'll give me the address, I'll head into town for a few supplies and then arrive in an hour or so. Will that do?"

She nodded. "*Jah*, that will be fine."

He glanced over the baked goods on the table next to her. "I'll take that apple pie," he said, pointing to the very pie that Katy had topped off with marmalade. He reached for his wallet in his back pocket. "How much?"

"Fifteen dollars," Naomi said, picking it up and handing it to him.

He gave her a twenty dollar bill. "Keep the change. And maybe you could serve it for dinner tonight?" he suggested. "Plus, I'll pay extra for the meals if needed."

She shook her head. "*Nee*. There's no extra charge for that." She smiled, thinking how surprised Ben would be to get a piece of apple pie for dinner after all.

After putting her address in his phone, Justin tipped his head in farewell, got into his car, and drove off. Naomi stood there unmoving, watching him drive away. What had she just done? Invited a stranger to spend the night at her house? She should be completely alarmed at her own nerve, but all she felt was grateful. God had given her another way to support themselves.

Her sisters and brothers back in Pennsylvania had been haranguing her for months to return home. They simply couldn't understand her reluctance to leave Hollybrook. After all, there was nothing there for her anymore. But they were wrong. Her *dat's* and her husband's dream was there. They had worked for years to make it happen. To find just the right land at just the right price. And they'd finally found it in Hollybrook, Indiana.

She refused to leave. Truth be told, in the beginning, she had considered selling, but when she'd investigated the possibility, she'd found that the economy had changed since their purchase. In that little bit of time, the price she could ask for the land wouldn't even cover the debt she owed.

And she wasn't about to leave Hollybrook with debt hanging over her head. It would be wrong and disrespectful of her father and her husband.

No. She was going to stay, and she was going to make it work. Besides, forcing yet another change on her children wouldn't be wise. She gazed up at the fluttering leaves of the oak tree above her head. Truth was, she couldn't bear to leave her husband there. Alone.

Tears burned her eyes as she thought of his body, lying deep in the warm earth. *Without her.*

"What would I do without you?" Isaac used to ask, tweaking her long hair over her shoulders as they sat up in bed together. "You're my life. My everything."

When he had said such things to her, a fleeting fear would pass through her, and she would shudder. Somehow, his devotion, his love, had seemed too strong, too encompassing, as if they were too much for this world. She couldn't explain it. Indeed, she hardly understood the feeling herself, but it was there. And now, seeing how it had turned out, how their love was killed in its prime, she wondered whether what she had felt was some kind of premonition. Some foretelling of the tragedy that was to come.

She moved to the side table and fussed with the embroidered tea towels, rearranging them to better effect. It did no good to ruminate on the past. It was the future that required all her energy and wisdom. It was the future that needed her planning and her courage.

"*Mamm!*" called Ben, running to the stand. "It's true! There's a big bumpy toad in Liz's tree. It's got warts all over it. It's soooo gross!"

His brown eyes sparkled with delight. Naomi laughed and ran her hand through his sweaty bangs. "Is that so?"

"Can I get a toad?"

"I don't think it works that way, Ben. Toads come and go as they please."

He clasped his hands together. "I hope one comes our way. I'm gonna name it Warty."

"Sounds like a right fine name." Naomi peered out from the stand, glancing down the road. "Where's your sister?"

"She's coming. She said it wasn't dark yet, and we didn't have to go, but I'm hungry."

"Mary should be back in a minute. So as soon as Katy shows up, we'll head for home."

No sooner had the words gone from her mouth than Mary arrived, huffing and stewing. "You were right, Naomi. I needed to check on things. Betty, bless her heart, was in the middle of burning a batch of biscuits. So, I guess we're eating burnt offerings tonight." She threw back her head and laughed. "That child! What am I to do? She'll never be able to keep a house."

Naomi chuckled along with her, but she was distracted. Should she tell Mary what she was about to do? Would Mary approve?

She decided against it. When the *Englisch* man's stay was successful, she would broach the subject. But should it not work out, she wouldn't have to say a thing. Only later would she realize the foolishness of such reasoning. She should have shared her plans with Mary then and there.

Katy skipped into the stand. "I'm hungry, *Mamm*."

"*Jah*, you're not the only one," Naomi said, nodding at Katy's brother. "Let's get in the cart and go on home." She turned to Mary. "Unless you still need my help."

Mary waved her hand in dismissal. "*Nee*. You all go on now. I'll bring you your money tomorrow evening some time."

"I sold one of the pies. Do I give you a portion of the price?"

Mary guffawed. "You're the one who helped me out today. Now, if it was a regular arrangement, I probably would take a portion at that. But not for a one-time event. Enjoy the profits."

"Thank you, Mary," Naomi said. Her eyes misted over, and she looked away in embarrassment. "I'll see you later then."

The children had already climbed into the cart, and Katy handed Naomi the reins when she got in. Naomi slapped them gently on Molly's back, and the mare started down the road. When they were out of earshot of Mary, Naomi turned to her children.

"We're having a guest for the next five nights. I'm counting on your help now."

"Who is it?" asked Ben.

"*Jah*, who's coming?" Katy chimed in.

"A gentleman named Justin Moore. He's—"

Katy interrupted her. "Is he *Englisch*?"

Naomi saw the look of alarm on her daughter's face. "*Jah*, but he's a nice man, Katy."

"Why's he staying with us?" Katy's voice had gone defensive. "*Dat* told us we shouldn't get friendly with the *Englisch*."

Naomi looked at her, trying to gauge the level of her upset. "Your *dat* only meant we should be cautious about becoming close friends with the *Englisch*, not that we shouldn't express kindness and courtesy. Anyway, this is a business arrangement. We could use the money."

"He's paying us?" Ben asked.

"We're opening a Bed and Breakfast." As the words passed her lips, Naomi realized her own conviction at the words. A feeling of peace settled over her, and she knew it was decided.

"A what?" Katy asked.

"A type of hotel. Where people pay you to spend the night, and you also feed them breakfast and perhaps some other meals."

"Where's he going to sleep? Is he going to sleep in *Dat's* place?" Katy's voice had risen to a high pitch.

Naomi yanked up on the reins, and the three of them nearly toppled off the bench seat as Molly came to an abrupt halt.

"*What?*" Naomi wheezed out in utter shock. "Whatever gave you that idea?"

Katy folded her arms in front of her chest and pressed her lips together.

"Katy Byler! What the world are you thinking? Of course, he's not. He'll be staying in the *daadi haus*."

Katy kept her eyes forward as if she hadn't heard a word Naomi had said.

"Katy," Naomi said, putting her hand on Katy's shoulder. "Look at me."

Slowly, Katy's gaze turned to her mother. Her look reminded Naomi of a hurt puppy, crouching in the corner.

"Katy," Naomi repeated her name, but much gentler this time. "We need to make money to take care of ourselves. You know that. This is a way for us to make money."

"What about the money that Zachariah gives you? He pays you every month! What about that?" Katy's voice was filled with tears, but her eyes remained wide and dry.

"*Jah*. And that's very helpful. But it's not enough."

"It should be! You just don't know how to manage money!" Katy accused, her voice sharp.

Naomi flinched. She would never have expected such a reaction from her daughter. She paused, debating how to respond, but no words came. In her heart of hearts, she wondered whether Katy was right. She *feared* Katy was right.

She swallowed hard and then slapped the reins again. Molly gave a lurch, and the pony cart rolled toward home. An awkward silence fell over the three of them, interrupted only with an occasional soft gasping breath from Katy. Naomi's mind reeled. Such disrespect in a child was not acceptable, but something within Naomi warned her to tread lightly. Katy was still not herself. She was still fragile.

When they pulled up to the barn, Ben jumped out. Katy followed, landing on the ground with a soft thud.

"You two take care of the cart and Molly. I need to go through the *daadi haus* to ensure all is ready. Then I'm going to need help with dinner."

Naomi climbed out of the cart and headed toward the *daadi haus*. Katy ran to catch up with her, pulling on her arm. Naomi stopped and looked at her daughter.

"I'm sorry, Mama." She looked at her feet. "I'll help you."

Naomi's heart went out to her. She touched her forearm gently. "I know you're sorry, Katy. And I'm counting on your help."

Katy glanced up then, her eyes welling with tears. "You're not mad?"

Naomi shook her head. "Let's forget it happened, shall we?"

Katy grabbed Naomi in a quick, fervent hug. Just as quickly, she released her and ran back to the pony cart to help Ben with Molly. Naomi fought her own tears. She pressed her hand to her chest and turned away to hurry to the *daadi haus*. She opened the door and immediately went to open each window, letting the late breeze waft through the small house. She glanced around, grateful that she'd left it so tidy when they'd moved their things to the big house. She entered the main bedroom. The double bed was neatly made up with clean sheets and one of her mother's favorite quilts. She stopped short, unable to move further into the room.

A wave of grief took hold of her, and she shook with the jolt of it. She grabbed the edge of the dresser and hung on, waiting for it to pass. The pain stormed through her chest and into her stomach, swirling there, before moving to her heart. She nearly buckled with it, squeezing her eyes shut and forcing herself to breathe.

This room. This was the place she and Isaac had dreamed and loved and shared everything. This room *was* Isaac. She backed up until she was pressed against the wall. What was she thinking to allow a stranger to sleep there?

Breathe, she told herself. *Breathe, Naomi. Slow and easy. You can do this.*

A crow's caw raked through the air outside, and she opened her eyes. She inched away from the wall until she was standing again on her own. She faltered, but stiffened herself to maintain her posture. No. She would not succumb again. It was only a room. Only a bed. It wasn't Isaac at all. She lurched across the floor to smooth the quilt, although it didn't need it. She glanced at the lantern on the bedside table and saw that matches were in reach.

Then with determined steps, she went to the bathroom and made sure fresh towels were in place. Everything was in order. There was no food in the kitchen, but Mr. Moore would join them for meals. Gulping back the dull pain in her throat, she left the *daadi haus* and moved somewhat mechanically to the big house. She entered through the side door and saw Katy already in the kitchen.

"I thought we could warm the stew," she said. "And there's enough bread to serve company I think."

Naomi went to her daughter and drew her close for a long hug. She felt Katy shudder in her arms, but only for a brief moment. She let her go and together, they bustled about the kitchen getting supper ready.

"Ben, set the plates, would you?"

Ben came in from the washroom, his hands still dripping. "Where should I put the *Englischer's* plate?"

Katy eyed Naomi. Naomi took a deep breath. "Put it next to your spot, Ben." She knew Katy was worried that the stranger would sit in her *dat's* or grandparents' spots. But no, Naomi wouldn't allow that, either.

A knock was heard on the front door. Naomi's brows rose. She hadn't heard a car drive in. She wiped her hands down her apron and rushed to the door. Opening it, she was startled to see Zachariah.

"Oh, Zachariah," she said, taking a quick breath. "I didn't know it was you."

He studied her for a moment. "Are you expecting company?"

"Well, *jah*. I mean, *nee*. Well, not company exactly."

Ben rushed up behind Naomi. "Hey, Mr. Zach! Guess what? We got an *Englischer* coming!"

Zach's gaze jerked to Naomi. He tilted his head, looking at her uncertainly. "What's this?"

Naomi squirmed under his gaze, which annoyed her. Why should she feel like she had to explain herself to him? He only leased her land. They had no relationship beyond that. Did they?

"I-I'm taking in boarders," she stammered. "This gentleman is here to write about the county fair."

The line of Zach's mouth tightened a fraction, and although he said nothing, she knew he was displeased. She saw the agitation in his eyes.

He turned away from the door and then paused, looking back. He stepped close, his eyes on hers.

"Did you need something?" Naomi asked, her hand on the screen.

"I wanted to know if you needed anything," he said. His voice was low and thick and melodious. "But I see you're busy."

She prickled at his words, unsure as to why she was suddenly annoyed. "*Jah*. Everything's fine," she answered, mildly surprised at her own curt tone.

He raised his hand and for a fleeting second, she thought he was going to touch her hand. Her eyes widened, and he froze. He cleared his throat and the look he gave her was full of feeling. She blinked, trying to read him.

But he had moved away again, going down the steps. He raised his hand in farewell.

"Bye, Mr. Zach!" Ben called. "See you tomorrow, okay?"

"*Jah,* Ben. See you tomorrow." But he didn't look back.

Ben scampered into the house, but Naomi hesitated a moment, watching Zach's wide-shouldered, rangy body disappear down the drive. She frowned, and a tremor touched her soft smooth lips. What had just happened?

Chapter Four

Naomi shook herself and forced herself to look away. She hadn't time to ponder the mysterious ways of Zachariah King. Justin Moore would be there any minute. And sure enough, as if her thoughts had conjured him up, he drove in at that precise moment. He must have passed Zachariah coming in. Justin parked his white sedan under the large poplar at the side of the house. She watched him unfold himself out of the car and reach into the backseat for his two bags. He grinned widely at her as he approached the porch.

"Howdy again, ma'am." He set his bags at her feet at the top of the porch. "Give me a minute."

He returned to his car and this time, he retrieved Naomi's apple pie from the passenger side of the car. "Can't forget about the pie now, can we? My mouth's been waterin' since I put it next to me on the seat. Fact is, I nearly ate it with my bare hands, it smelled so good."

Naomi laughed and set the pie on the small porch table. "I do have forks, Mr. Moore. Don't you worry."

He stood before her. "I'm not worried," he said, his voice soft. "I'm not worried about a single thing."

She took a step back, startled at his familiar tone.

Ben burst through the screen door. When he saw Justin, he stopped short, suddenly turning shy. Naomi reached out and took Ben's shoulder. "This is my son, Benjamin," she said.

"Howdy, Benjamin," Justin said. He grinned. "You look like a strapping farmer to me."

Ben looked up at their tall visitor, a proud glow coming to his cheeks. "I help a lot around here," he said.

"I imagine you do. It's mighty fine for a mother to have such a son."

Naomi fidgeted a bit with the seam of Ben's shirt, feeling uncomfortable with how forward this *Englischer* seemed. But upon looking into Justin's gleaming eyes, she decided that there was only friendliness there. She'd heard of the outspoken ways of the *Englischers*.

"Your quarters are around back," she said, making a move to grab one of his bags. "I'll show you to them."

"I'll carry my own bags, ma'am," he said with a chuckle. "Around back, you say?"

"*Jah*. In our *daadi haus*."

"*Daadi haus?*"

She smiled as he matched her stride. "We Amish most always have a *daadi haus* behind the main house or sometimes even adjoining the main house. Our parents stay there when they grow older, and one of their children moves into the main house with their brood." She shrugged. "Or, at times, a newlywed couple will stay in the *daadi haus*."

"Or in your case, a mighty curious stranger," he finished for her and laughed.

She climbed the steps of the small house and pulled open the screen door. He walked in with her, and his very presence filled the room. She caught her breath, a heady feeling swooping over her. It was all wrong —another man walking through that door. And it was all wrong—

another man fixing to stay there. *Sleep there.* In the very bed she had shared with Isaac. With a quick change of heart, she showed Justin Moore to what had been her children's bedroom, with two single beds pushed up against opposite walls. Her face was burning, and she knew her cheeks were bright pink.

But she couldn't do it. She couldn't show him to the room she had shared with her husband. She couldn't bear the thought of him, this stranger, climbing into *their* bed.

"Why, this looks mighty nice," Justin said with an appreciative nod.

"There's a lantern on the table right there with matches. There are also lanterns in the main room should you need them."

Justin set his two bags on one of the beds. He glanced down at the quilt that was pulled tightly over the mattress with neat corners tucked in at the end. "Did you make this?"

Her cheeks grew warmer still. "*Jah.*"

He leaned down and ran his hand over the soft piecework with the small even stitches. "It's beautiful. Of course, the Amish are known for their quilts." He stood, and she again marveled at his height. "But I've never known the actual seamstress."

She shook her head. "It's nothing special," she murmured. "Every woman worth her salt knows how to do the same."

"You're wrong," he said, his voice gentle. "It's very special, indeed."

She blew out her breath and took a step toward the door. Her legs felt a bit wobbly, and she was ashamed at the effect this man seemed to have on her. She was on edge, feeling exactly how she used to feel as a girl when she walked along the top of the fence surrounding their front yard. One tiny misstep, and she'd go tumbling down to the dirt.

"Supper will be on the table in a half hour," she said, her voice all business. "If you need anything further, you let me or one of the children know."

"Children?"

"*Jah*. My daughter Katy is inside. She's eleven."

He smiled. "I look forward to meeting her." He bent down to unzip one of his bags, and he pulled out a computer. "It's all charged and ready to go. I found a fast food joint not far from here, too, where I can recharge it when I need to."

She blinked and nodded. "All right, then. We'll see you inside for supper."

She turned and practically fled from the *daadi haus*, not sure why she felt such a compulsion to get out of there so fast. Mr. Moore was a nice man, friendly and engaging. She hurried to the side door of the big house and paused. It wasn't really Mr. Moore she was fleeing. It was the *daadi haus*. That place. That place where she'd been happy and excited and grateful to be starting a new chapter of her life with Isaac. Where she'd been eager to fit in and make friends in Hollybrook.

Had she made a mistake? Was she not ready to have guests? Even paying ones? She blew out her breath. Her being ready was not important. What was important was that in five days, Mr. Moore was going to hand her five hundred dollars. Money that would buy food and supplies and chicken feed. Money that would ease her worries.

She squared her shoulders and put on a smile. Walking inside and through the washroom to the kitchen, she greeted her children. "Katy, I told Mr. Moore we'd be ready in a half hour. How's the stew coming?"

Katy gave another stir to the large pot on the stove. "Already warm, *Mamm*."

"Wonderful."

"He's so tall," Ben said.

"That he is, son."

"Are all *Englischers* so tall?"

Katy scoffed. "Course they're not. They're regular humans just like us."

Ben made a face at his sister and wandered toward the dining area.

37

"Now, I don't want any of that at the dinner table," Naomi scolded. "You'll both be on your best behavior, you hear?"

"*Jah*, Mama," Ben muttered.

"Should I dish up the stew?" Katy asked.

"*Nee*. Let's wait a few more minutes, or it'll go cold again. I'll get the milk poured."

"Should we make some tea?"

Naomi regarded her daughter. "Katy girl, you're going to surpass me sooner than I thought. That's a right fine idea. I'll put the kettle on."

In a half hour on the nose, Justin Moore knocked on the front door. Naomi rushed to answer it. "Oh Mr. Moore, you can use the side door," she said.

"I didn't know which one I should use. I figured the front door was a safe bet." He walked into the front room and glanced around.

"Please come through," Naomi coaxed. "We're ready for you."

He walked into the dining area. Katy and Ben stood at the side of the table staring at him.

"Hello, Benjamin," he said and smiled at Ben.

"You can call me Ben."

"All right, be glad to, Ben." He gazed at Katy. "And you must be Katy."

Katy looked a bit awestruck as she stared at their guest. But Naomi knew her well, and she could see the wheels of judgment turning in her daughter's mind. For some reason, Katy seemed predisposed to dislike Mr. Moore. Naomi would have to ask her about it later.

"You're gonna sit by me," Ben said, slipping onto the long wooden bench and pointing to the spot next to him.

"That's just where I was hoping to sit," Justin said, climbing onto the bench. His legs were so long that it took a bit of maneuvering to get them under the table.

Katy sat opposite him, and Naomi sat at the head spot. The week before she'd decided that someone needed to preside over the table, and it fell to her to do it. She clasped her hands on her lap. "Shall we pray?" she asked a bit nervously, wondering how Justin would react.

But she needn't have worried. Smooth as a whistle, Justin folded his hands and bowed his head. Naomi sent up a silent prayer for wisdom and guidance in this new venture. She thanked God for sending the opportunity her way, and vowed that she would do her utmost to please Him with her efforts. She prayed a bit longer than usual, and she sensed Ben beginning to fidget. She coughed and the three of them raised their heads, the prayer over. Justin still had his head bowed.

"We're done, mister," Ben declared.

"Benjamin!" scolded Naomi. "You must never interrupt someone at prayer. It isn't seemly."

Justin looked up and blinked a few times. "No problem. I'm finished." He gazed at the food on the table. "My, it all smells so fine."

"My *mamm* makes the best stew around," Ben said, digging his spoon deeply into his bowl.

"I'm sure that's the truth. Ms. Byler, did you remember the pie for dessert?"

Ben gulped down his bite and dropped his spoon with a clatter. "You mean I get pie after all?"

Naomi laughed. "Mr. Moore bought one of my pies at Mary's roadside stand. We're having it for dessert."

"An apple one?" Ben asked. "Tell me it's an apple one."

Justin leaned his head down to Ben's level. "It's an apple one."

"Yippee!" Ben said. He grabbed up his spoon and took another huge bite of stew.

Katy watched, her face devoid of expression. She ate with dainty bites, and her posture was stiff as a fence post.

"Katy, what kinds of things are you interested in?" Justin asked between mouthfuls.

Katy sucked in her lips and looked at her mother. Naomi nodded at her.

"I-I don't know exactly what you mean," she stammered.

"I was just wondering what kinds of hobbies you're interested in. Or what sports or activities."

"Sports?" she looked again at Naomi and then back at Mr. Moore. "We play softball and tag at school."

"That sounds fun," he said. He seemed at a loss then, as if he'd suddenly realized how different an Amish child's life was, and he wasn't sure which direction his small talk should take.

"The children and youth like corner ball," Naomi offered.

"Corner ball?"

"It's a bit like dodge ball, except we play with a small hard ball. We cover the play field with straw so it doesn't hurt so much when you fall."

"A small hard ball? Ouch!"

"*Jah!* One time Amos Criter fell and broke his wrist. 'Member that, *Mamm*? Back at our old house?" Ben's eyes danced with the memory. "And then he had to go to a doctor. An *Englisch* one? 'Member?"

"I remember, son. But please don't sound so excited about someone else's hardship."

Ben bowed his head. "Sorry," he mumbled.

"We got to write our names on his cast," Katy offered, looking semi-interested in the conversation for the first time.

"More stew?" Naomi asked Justin.

He handed her his bowl. "If it's not too much trouble."

40

She took his bowl and stood. "Of course, it's not." She went into the kitchen and dipped him another full bowl. Returning to the table, she placed it before him. "Can I get you anything else?"

"Nope. Not until the pie." He elbowed Ben, who giggled.

Someone knocked on the door. Naomi's eyes widened. Who could that be? Katy jumped up. "I'll get it for you, *Mamm*."

She hurried away from the table, and Naomi heard her open the front door. "Mr. Zachariah," Katy said. "Do you need something?"

Zachariah? Again?

This was a full-out record. Never once in all these months had Zachariah come to the door more than once a week at best. And here he was for the *third* time on the same day?

Naomi got up from the table. "Excuse me, please." She wiped her hands on her apron and went to the door.

"*Mamm*, I asked Mr. Zachariah to join us for a piece of pie," Katy said with a look of boldness.

Naomi frowned, wondering just what her daughter was thinking. But then, if she knew Zachariah, he would never agree. In the past, he hadn't set foot in the house for so much as a glass of water.

Zachariah gave a slow nod. "I'd be pleased to join you," he said.

Naomi nearly grunted in surprise, but she recovered quickly. "Why then, come on through. We're just about ready to serve it."

Zachariah followed her and Katy into the dining area. Katy had suddenly gone mute and an awkward silence filled the air. Justin looked up with curiosity when Zach walked in.

"Mr. King, this is Mr. Moore. He's boarding with us for a few days." Naomi felt a further urge to explain herself but resisted. She didn't owe any explanations to Zachariah King.

The two men eyed each other. Zachariah's face had gone dark, and he wore an almost threatening look. Justin's eyes narrowed ever so slightly, and Naomi saw him swallow. Then he smiled and offered Zach his hand. With a cold stare, Zachariah shook it.

Naomi gaped at them both. If she didn't know better, she'd say Zachariah was jealous. Inwardly, she scoffed. Her imagination was going wild, taking her to ridiculous places.

She looked at her daughter. "Katy, get Mr. King a plate and bring the pie out, will you? Would anyone like some tea?"

"No ma'am, not for me," Justin said. He stood and picked up his dinner plate and bowl.

"What are you doing?" Ben asked.

"Taking my dishes out to the kitchen," he said with a wink.

Naomi rushed to him and took the dishes from his hands. "*Nee.* You mustn't do that, Mr. Moore. You sit back down and wait for your pie."

"Men don't do dishes," Ben muttered, giving Justin a suspicious look.

"Don't they now? My mom taught me differently." Justin's rich laugh rang through the room.

Zachariah sat at the end of the table in the chair usually used by Isaac. When Katy returned with pie plates for them all, her face turned red as she observed him sitting there. Zachariah must have noticed her reaction, for he stood halfway up. "Did you want me to sit elsewhere?" he asked.

Katy shook her head. "*Nee,* it's all right. Here's your plate." She turned and dashed back to the kitchen, bringing the pie out.

Zach settled back down, looking both relieved and pleased.

"So, no one would like any tea?" Naomi asked again, wondering how her perfectly nice supper had disintegrated into such an uncomfortable, stilted affair.

"I'd like some," Zachariah said. "If it's not too much bother."

"Of course it isn't any bother," Naomi said, forcing a cheerful smile.

Suddenly, she just wanted everyone to go away and leave her be. Even her children. She yearned for time alone, maybe to curl up in bed under the comfort of her own warm quilt.

She gave a soft snort at such foolish thinking. She took the whistling kettle off the stove and poured hot water into a large mug. Before she dropped in the teabag, Justin came into the room, carrying the basket of bread.

"Mr. Moore, please sit back down."

He set the basket on the counter and regarded her. "Are you all right?"

Naomi felt sudden heat flash across her face. Could the man see right through her? She placed the teabag in the water with an unsteady hand. "*Jah*, I'm fine."

He glanced around quickly and spotted the bowl of sugar next to the salt shaker. He picked it up and handed it to her. His hand brushed hers with an electrifying jolt and a warning voice whispered in her head. She jerked back, up against the counter. She blanched, wondering at her reaction.

His eyes were on her, and he gave her a kind smile. "I didn't know if Mr. King preferred sugar or not."

Naomi raised her chin. "I wouldn't know." Her voice was clipped, and she became very official as she bustled back out to the table. "Here you are, Mr. King."

She set the mug and the bowl of sugar down next to his plate with such force, the hot water slopped over the side of the cup, burning her fingers. She snatched them back and sudden tears flooded her eyes. Mortified, she blinked rapidly and hurried to the head of the table. "Now then, shall we have some pie," she said, grateful that her voice came out normally.

She cut and dished up the pie, thankful that Ben had started a conversation about tree toads. Zachariah entered right in with his apparent many years of frog and toad experience. Ben was all grins when Zach told him about a "pet" frog he once kept in a shoebox. Until his *mamm* found out, of course.

Katy was unusually quiet, and when her last bite was eaten, she nearly raced to escape with the dishes to the kitchen. Naomi had never known her so eager to clear away the table. Justin followed Zach's and Ben's conversation, but didn't offer any comments. Naomi felt him look at her more than once, and she stubbornly kept her eyes on her son.

When Zach got up to leave, she nearly burst into tears with relief. Along with Ben, she walked him to the door.

"Benjamin, for goodness sakes, let go of the man's arm. He needs to go."

Ben dropped Zach's arm. "Sorry." He looked at his mother. "But he's gonna show me where the tree frogs usually hide."

"That's all fine and *gut*, but we mustn't keep him from his duties."

Zach ran his hand over Ben's head, musing his hair. "My duties?" he questioned, looking over Ben at her. His eyes were gentle and contemplative, and she found herself unable to look away. It was as if something connected the two of them, something fragile and tenuous, but there all the same. "My duties are farming," he said. His voice was soft, almost tender, and the sound caressed her. "And it's dark."

Naomi clasped her hands together and pressed them to her chest, feeling completely unsettled. Her breathing grew shallow and quick.

"You won't forget?" Ben said, snapping Naomi back to the moment.

Zach grinned down at him. "I'll show you tomorrow afternoon, if you'd like. No promises, though. Sometimes those frogs are mighty hard to spot."

"Tomorrow?" Ben asked, a huge smile on his face. "Okay."

Zach stepped outside and put on his straw hat. He nodded to Naomi, holding her gaze for a moment longer than necessary. "Thank you for the pie. It was *gut*."

She blinked and took a deep breath. "You're welcome."

He turned and left, strolling slowly as if he had all the time in the world. When he disappeared into the growing darkness, she realized that he hadn't told her why he'd stopped by in the first place that evening.

But he hadn't needed to—she *knew*. He was checking out her guest. Assessing the situation.

She shut the door and ran her hand along the satiny oak wood, lost in thought. It had been a long day, and she was ready for it to be over.

"Ma'am?" It was Justin.

She turned. "*Jah?*"

"I'll be turning in, then. Thank you for a delicious meal. And the pie..." He bunched his fingers to his lips and gave them a kiss, spreading his fingers wide. "Delicious!"

She frowned and then couldn't help but grin at the look of contentment on his face. "Thank you," she murmured.

"Good night," he said. He motioned toward the washroom with his head. "The side door?"

She nodded. "The side door."

He left the room then, heading through the washroom to the side door. Before leaving the house, he looked back to where she stood, watching him.

Chapter Five

After the children were tucked in for the night, Naomi sat on her bed staring at the flickering light from the lantern. It played against the walls of her room, dancing and casting long, misshapen shadows. She reached into her bedside table and pulled out her tablet and pencil. She scooted back against the headboard and flipped through the pages full of her scrawled words. After the accident, she'd taken to keeping a journal of sorts. She'd had no one to talk to. No one to listen. She could hardly cry out her grief to her children. They had unimaginable depths of their own grief.

Her family hadn't come to the funerals. Nor had Isaac's siblings. Naomi truly thought they'd wanted to, but the trip from Pennsylvania was too long, too expensive, and the funerals took place two days after the crash. Afterwards, her brothers had begged her to come back to Pennsylvania to live. Her elder brother Marvin had been quite relentless. But so had Naomi.

She simply couldn't fathom another massive change to her life. She simply couldn't. So she limped through the days in a foggy haze, crying whenever the children weren't within earshot, and holding them when they were.

She resisted the temptation to reread all she'd written in those first few weeks. It only served to make the pain sharper. And she was tired of it. Weary beyond words. She ached for a new beginning. Something she could look forward to. Something to be glad about.

She began writing.

Today marks the first day of the Byler Bed and Breakfast. We have our first guest. He's a journalist and a nice man.

She paused. And erased.

He's a journalist. He's covering the county fair. Writing articles and such. I am charging him one hundred dollars a night, and he's staying for five. I believe the children are all right with this new endeavor. Katy seems troubled, but I think it's mostly because nobody has really been in the house except us since the accident. Perhaps I should have spoken with both of them first, but the opportunity was so quick and unexpected, that I leapt at it.

I have wondered what Isaac would think.

Nee. I can't keep doing this. Isaac is gone. He doesn't think anything.

Zachariah King stopped by three times today. That is odd. And it troubled me. He made me nervous somehow. One time, during the evening, I wondered if he had interest in me. But, nee. Sometimes I don't trust my own judgment. But the good news is he will continue to lease the land. I think that if I can get enough guests, and Zach keeps leasing, things will be all right. That is my prayer anyway.

I'm tired. So tired. I'll write more tomorrow.

Naomi closed her notebook and placed it back in the drawer with her pencil. She snuffed out the lantern and snuggled down in her bed. It was a bit stuffy to be under the covers, but she found the quilt so comforting that she left it on. Within minutes, she was asleep.

Early the next morning, Naomi hurried out to the chicken coop to gather eggs. Normally, Katy did the job, but she wasn't up and about yet. Naomi realized that she hadn't discussed the hour for breakfast with Mr. Moore the night before, so she wanted to be ready extra early in case he needed to leave for the day soon.

There was a heavy layer of dew on the ground, and her bare feet left wet footprints on the wood base just inside the coop. The wood gave way to dirt and straw though, and Naomi picked her way carefully to the roosting slots. The hens sent up a flurry of dust as they flapped their wings at her arrival. Three of the hens ran crazily around the perimeter, scolding her every move. Naomi laughed at their antics as she collected the eggs.

"You silly hens," she said. "Quit your fussing. I'll get your feed soon enough."

"I thought I heard something," came a deep voice from outside the pen.

Naomi swirled around and saw Justin grinning at her. "Mr. Moore! You're up. I'm so sorry. Breakfast isn't ready yet."

He waved his hand. "No worries. I haven't even jogged."

"Jogged?"

"My daily run." He looked at a band on his wrist. "I should be back and showered in an hour. Would that be all right for breakfast?"

"Of course." One of the hens pecked at her toes, and she did a small hip hop dance to get away.

Justin laughed. "You're mighty brave going in there with no shoes on."

Naomi shrugged. "They mean no harm. They're quite friendly, actually."

"Are they now?"

Naomi put another two eggs in her basket.

"Can I help?" he asked.
"What? You want to gather eggs?"

"Never done it before."

She stared at him as if he wasn't a normal person. "Never?"

"Nope." He opened the screened door and stepped inside. He flinched a bit at the new flurry of excitement his entry caused. "Whoa! Maybe they don't like males."

Naomi laughed. "Ah, they just know you haven't a clue as to what you're doing."

"You got that right."

"Come over here. I haven't checked those two slots yet. And usually our best layers roost there. Just dig a bit in the straw."

Justin shooed one of the hens away, and then he reached in and his eyes lit up. "They're still warm!"

Naomi watched his pleasure with a chuckle. Seeing a grown man excited over finding warm eggs in a chicken coop was an unknown concept to her. She couldn't get over the fact that this fancy man hadn't a lick of practical experience.

"Here," he said proudly, putting three eggs in the basket. "And there's more. Just a sec..." He dug around and found four more eggs in the slots. He looked so pleased, you'd have thought he'd produced them himself.

"Good job, Mr. Moore."

"Are we going to eat these eggs for breakfast? The ones I found?"

"We are. How would you like them? Scrambled or fried or boiled?"

"Would fried, sunny-side up, be too much trouble?"

"Mr. Moore, you are my paying guest. It's not too much trouble. I'll fry up some bacon, too, and Katy will make up the toast. I've got different types of preserves. Would blackberry do?"

He stood there in the middle of a flock of pecking hens with a look of sheer delight on his face. "It will do fine," he said. "Thank you."

She laughed again and shook her head. "You're easy to please." She opened the door of the coop, and he followed her out. "Breakfast will be ready for you in an hour."

"Sounds good," he said and took off at a jog. She watched him as he ran down the drive and onto the road. She would never understand the *Englisch* person's penchant for exercising. She got plenty of physical activity by simply going about her chores for the day. She couldn't imagine adding a morning run for the sole purpose of exercise.

Katy was slicing a loaf of bread when Naomi returned with the eggs. "Thank you, Katy girl. We'll serve Mr. Moore breakfast in an hour."

"An hour? Why so late?"

"He's exercising. Jogging about the county from what I can tell."

"Jogging about the county? That's crazy."

"Watch your tone, daughter. We have to be respectful."

"I don't like him." Katy pursed her lips into a tight grimace.

Naomi set the basket of eggs on the counter and studied her. "Why not? He's a perfectly nice person."

"He likes you."

"What?"

Katy set the knife down and swallowed. "Do you like him?"

Naomi's cheeks went hot. "What a perfectly ridiculous thing to say." She bent down and opened a cupboard, yanking out her iron skillet. "And I'll thank you for minding your words from now on. Your father may not be here, but I am your mother."

"I know *Dat's* not here!" Katy cried, her lips trembling. "You don't have to remind me!"

And with that, she flew from the kitchen and out the side door, slamming it behind her. Naomi stared after her, her mouth open and her eyes wide. Then with a sigh, she picked up the knife and finished slicing the bread. Her mind spun through her options. Should she go find Katy and comfort the child? Should she wait until Katy returned and have a talk with her? Should she discipline her daughter for such rudeness to her elder?

Naomi sank onto one of the kitchen chairs. She rested an elbow on the table and leaned her chin in her hand. It was only early morning, and already she was exhausted. And where was Ben? She glanced behind her, through the kitchen door toward the staircase. He was probably still asleep, and the dairy cow needed seeing to. She blew out her breath. She supposed she could take care of that, too. She couldn't cook the eggs yet anyway.

She stood and smoothed down her apron. She would talk to Katy when she returned, but she'd go easy on her. Naomi knew only too well how hard it was to lose someone you loved. It changed you. And not always for the best.

She put a dishtowel over the sliced loaf of bread and headed back outside toward the barn.

Breakfast went well. Immediately after eating, Justin Moore left in his car for town. Interviews, he told her.

Katy had shown up for breakfast, looking submissive and contrite. Naomi gave her a quick hug and felt Katy's body relax into hers. "I'm sorry, *Mamm*," Katy murmured into Naomi's shoulder. "Again."

Naomi simply squeezed her daughter and then let her go to sit and eat. Katy insisted on doing all the clean-up. Naomi let her, knowing it would make her feel better.

Ben had raced out to the fields to see if he could find Zachariah, remembering Zach's promise of frog-hunting. Naomi reminded him that Zach had said in the afternoon, but Ben ran off just the same. The house was quiet, with only the sounds of Katy fussing about in the kitchen. Naomi eyed the basket of mending that sat next to the warming stove in the front room. It was full to overflowing. She hadn't mended for weeks, or was it months?

She grabbed it up along with her sewing supplies and took the work outside to the front porch. The morning was clear, and the sun had already burned off the dew. It was a perfect day to sit on the porch and mend. She lowered herself into the rocker and set the basket of clothes next to her. She pulled out one of Katy's everyday dresses and threaded a needle to work on the side seam which had ripped when the girl had climbed up to the barn loft. The dress had caught on a nail and split wide open.

Naomi chuckled, knowing that Katy would have been going too quickly to stop the rip before it became huge. The girl was always in a hurry, even when there was no need.

Naomi was halfway through the mending job when she saw Mary coming down her drive, her pony taking it at quite a clip. Naomi's heart sped up. Maybe Mary needed more pies. If she went to the store right away, she could get more ingredients and have the pies to Mary by that afternoon.

"Mary!" she called, standing and letting her mending fall to the ground. "Good morning."

When she caught sight of Mary's face up close, her heart sank. This visit had nothing to do with pies.

"What's wrong?" she asked, hurrying down the steps to meet her. "What's happened?"

Mary gave a huffing wheeze as she climbed out of her cart. She threw the pony's reins over the hitching rail and faced Naomi. "Can we sit a spell?" she asked.

"Why, of course. Can I get you some water or some tea? I might have some lemons left to make lemonade."

Mary sloughed her off with a wave of her arm. "*Nee*. Don't bother. Let's sit."

The two women sat in rocking chairs, and Naomi swallowed. Mary was making her nervous. What had happened?

"Is it true?" Mary asked, her voice frank. She brushed impatiently at the scraggly wisps of hair that had escaped her *kapp*.

"Is what true?"

"You had *Englischers* here all night?"

Naomi flinched. "What? Well, *jah*, but—"

"Who are they? And was it a man? Or was there a woman with him?" Mary interrupted her.

Naomi tensed, and she worked not to feel angry with such a line of questioning. "It was a gentleman journalist who is covering the county fair."

Mary's eyebrows rose. "What's he doing staying with you? Do you know him?"

"I do now." She took a long breath. "I'm opening a Bed and Breakfast."

"*What?*"

"You know, a sort of boarding house."

"Does Bishop know?"

Naomi's bravado seeped out in a low breath. "*Nee*." How foolish was she? She hadn't even thought to gain the bishop's permission or blessing. And here she'd entertained the thought of rewiring the house for electricity. What was the matter with her? How ignorant could she be?

"*Ach*, Naomi, what were you thinking?" Mary's tone turned sympathetic, and she patted Naomi's hand.

"I was thinking that it would be a good way to make money," she said.

"But, taking in *Englischers?*"

"They pay."

Mary bristled at that. "So do Amish!"

Naomi shook her head. "That's not what I meant. But how many guests am I going to have if I only board Amish folks? I'd have no one. They'd stay with relatives in the district."

"Well, you're right at that." Mary began rocking, and her chair creaked against the wide porch floorboards.

"How did you know?"

"Betsy Radcliff saw the car, and one question led to another. Everyone knows, dear girl, and I think you're going to hear about it."

Naomi jumped up, stepping on Katy's half-mended dress. "Oh, my!"

"Listen, it was an honest mistake. I can go to the bishop with you." Mary grinned in a conspiratorial way. "He looks kindly on me. I once helped his wife give birth when the midwife was tending someone else." She laughed and slapped her knee. "That was a time! For the bishop's wife to take second place..." She shook her head. "All done in innocence, though."

"You'll go with me? Do you think he'll give his permission?"

"I've heard tell of other Amish Bed and Breakfast outfits in other districts. I don't see why Hollybrook can't have one."

Naomi's breath trickled out. "I didn't intend to disturb anyone."

"Of course, you didn't," Mary said. "I'm sorry about my harshness earlier. I was worried. That's why I hightailed it over here."

"I know. And thank you." A sudden thought grabbed Naomi. Was this why Zachariah had shown up the night before? Had he intentionally been present at dinner to allay gossip? To ensure that she hadn't had dinner with the *Englischer* alone?

Was he trying to *help* her?

Mary swatted at a pesky fly buzzing about her head. "Can you go with me now? Bishop is probably working in his fields, but he'll come in if we show up over there."

Naomi glanced down at her dress. "Let me change into something clean, and I'll be right with you. And I have to tell Katy to watch Ben."

"Go on with you, then. I'll wait in the cart."

Chapter Six

Naomi hurried into the house and upstairs. Once again, she wondered at her reasoning powers of late. She should have gone to the bishop immediately with her idea. She didn't know the bishop very well; although, she had found him most sympathetic after the accident. He knew her situation. He also knew she could have returned to Pennsylvania but had chosen to stay in Hollybrook. Surely, he would be on board with her new plan.

She put on her for-good dress and glanced at herself in the hand mirror on her dresser. Her eyes had lost some of their haunted look, but she still looked tired. Would she ever regain her sparkling eyes and rosy cheeks? She put the mirror down and gave herself a scolding. Worrying about physical appearance was vanity, and she needed to stop it.

Still, when she ran back downstairs to tell Katy, the yearning for her former countenance remained.

Mary chatted animatedly all the way to the bishop's farm. Naomi tried to focus on her friend's conversation, but her mind was flying in all directions. She thought of Isaac and hoped he was smiling down at her. She thought of Katy's latest upset and knew that she'd be all right given more time. She thought of Ben and his upcoming frog adventure.

She thought of Zachariah and the fact that he would continue leasing from her. She thought of the burning look in his eyes when he'd left her the night before. And she thought of Justin Moore. Her breath caught as she visualized his gentle expression when he'd asked her how she was during dinner.

She clasped her hands firmly in her lap. Right after the accident, she had seen no way that her life could possibly work out. She'd seen no way to support her children or eke out a life for herself. She'd seen no way that she would survive, let alone have any joy.

But there she was, riding in a pony cart with a new and dear friend. There she was, going to the bishop's farm to ask his blessing on a business endeavor that she could manage. Maybe she didn't look like the same Naomi as before. Maybe she wasn't as comely. But did that really matter?

The closer they got to the Schrock's farm, the calmer Naomi grew. She marveled that her nervousness had died, and in its place was a calm assurance. The bishop was going to agree. Maybe not with the electricity, and in fact, she decided quickly that she wouldn't even mention the idea. After all, she'd gotten one guest without it. But the bishop would see the practicality of her idea of a Bed and Breakfast.

She looked at Mary. "Thank you."

"*Ach*, you already thanked me." Mary laughed and slapped the reins on her pony again.

Naomi shut her eyes and gave herself over to the gentle sway of the cart as it rolled down the road. She felt the sunshine on her face and heard the chickadees twitter in the trees as they passed. Mary turned the cart into the Schrock's drive, and the pony trotted right up to the front porch. Lois Schrock was at the side of the house, hanging up two dripping dishtowels.

"Good morning, Lois!" called Mary, waving.

Lois grinned and ambled over to them. "Why, Mary. And Naomi. A good morning to you both."

"We're here to speak with the bishop, if that's possible."

Lois shielded her eyes from the morning sun and gazed out toward the field. "I can send young Amos to get him," she said. "Bishop's due for a mid-morning break, anyway."

The three women headed for the rocking chairs on the porch.

"Can I get you some ice tea?" Lois asked.

"Sounds *gut*," Mary said, nodding.

Naomi agreed, settling back into one of the rockers to wait for the bishop as Lois disappeared into the house. Within minutes, Lois had returned with a tray holding a pitcher and four glasses of ice tea. And not long after that, Bishop appeared, wiping his hands down his trousers and taking off his straw hat.

"Good morning, ladies" he said. For such a wiry man, his voice was surprisingly strong and resonant. He mounted the steps and sank with a sigh into the empty rocker. Mary and Naomi both returned his greeting.

Lois handed him a glass of tea, and he gulped it down, placing his empty glass back on the tray. "What can I do for you, Mary?"

Mary leaned forward in her chair. "It's nothing for me, Bishop. It's for Naomi." She nodded at Naomi.

Before Mary could continue, Bishop clucked his tongue and regarded Naomi. "I'm glad you're here, Naomi. I was planning to talk with you later, myself."

Naomi's throat tightened. So he'd heard, too. She pressed her lips together.

"So what's this I hear about you entertaining *Englisch* guests?"

"That's why we're here. What Naomi's doing is—" Mary interjected quickly, but Naomi put her hand on Mary's arm, stopping her narrative.

"Bishop, I want to apologize for not seeking your guidance in the first place," Naomi said, her tone both contrite and confident. "I never intended to go over your head. You must know that I'm struggling with my finances—"

Lois gave a sharp intake of breath, and Bishop tossed her a censuring look.

"Anyway, I thought that if I opened a Bed and Breakfast, it would be a way to stay in Hollybrook. A way that I could make money."

"Doesn't Zachariah King lease your land?" Bishop asked.

"*Jah*, he does. But it's not enough. There's a mortgage."

"The district has funds," Bishop explained, a kind look on his face. "Those funds are to help our people who need it. Now, for medical emergencies, we often can cover the full cost."

Naomi nodded. "I know that, and I think it's a blessing. But, Bishop, this isn't a one-time expense. I need ongoing money to take care of my family."

"But Zachariah—" Lois began, but her husband interrupted her.

"I understand. So what you're asking for is a blessing to open a Bed and Breakfast."

"*Jah*."

"Are you planning to have electricity?"

Naomi swallowed. "*Nee*. Not at this point."

He nodded and his damp brown hair stuck to his forehead in clumps. "A phone?"

"That might be necessary."

"It wouldn't be the first phone in the district used for business," he said.

Naomi smiled. She'd been right—he was going to agree, she knew it. "Is it all right, then?"

He tugged on his long beard and regarded her. "I believe that God has given you this opportunity. And we're grateful you want to stay in Hollybrook."

Naomi's breath gushed out. "Thank you, Bishop. Thank you."

Mary gave a single clap and beamed as if she'd personally brought it all about.

"Now, if you'll excuse me, I need to get back to the fields." Bishop looked at his wife. "Send Amos back out, would you, Lois? I'll be needing him."

Lois agreed, and the bishop took his leave.

Naomi smiled at her two friends in relief. Mary gave her arm a squeeze. "See, Naomi? It's all working out fine."

Lois stood and picked up the pitcher of tea. She topped off both Naomi's and Mary's glasses. "So, how are you finding Zachariah?" she asked, looking directly at Naomi.

Naomi squirmed. "What do you mean?"

"How do you find him?"

"He's nice," Naomi answered, wondering just where this conversation was heading. "And he's responsible."

Lois sat down in her chair and adjusted her apron over her dress. "I've always liked that young man. He's got a lot of promise, that one."

Naomi nodded, growing suspicious of the woman's motivation.

"He'll make someone a mighty good husband," Lois continued.

And there it was... Mary must have sensed Naomi's discomfort because she took another sip of tea and stood. "We should get going, Lois. Thank you so much for the tea."

Naomi jumped up, too, and handed her glass to Lois. "*Jah*, thank you for the tea."

Lois blinked, looking disgruntled to have her conversation cut short.

"Y-You're welcome. And do come again. Anytime at all."

Mary bustled Naomi down the steps. They climbed into the cart and with a wave, were on their way within minutes.

"See there, Naomi," Mary said, nudging her friend as they reached the main road. "We have a very reasonable bishop in our district. He's well-loved, all right."

"I can see why."

"And Lois was right, you know," Mary continued. "Zachariah King is a fine man. Someday, I'll tell you his story."

Naomi's brow rose. "His story?"

Mary nodded and clicked her tongue at her pony, urging her on.

Zachariah's story. Naomi surprised herself by how much she wanted to hear it. Truth be told, she had more than a passing interest in Zachariah's story.

But not now. Now, she wanted to revel in the new feeling of hope that bubbled within her. She wanted to revel in the absence of pain and grief, however temporary it might be. She wanted to revel in the knowledge that the bishop had approved her plan.

She *would* hear Zachariah's story. But later.

She closed her eyes and let the hot morning sun bathe her face. The feeling of peace that had filled her in the cart ride over, remained. She breathed deeply and thanked God for her fledgling Bed and Breakfast. She thanked God for Mary and the sun and the healing that was coming to her and her children.

She opened her eyes and looked up to the clouds with a smile that was deep and beautiful. She was full to overflowing with anticipation for the future. She had a new business and new hope. For the first time in a *very* long time, Naomi believed that everything was going to be all right.

The End

THE ENGLISCHER
STAYED TWICE

Chapter One

Fear thou not; for I am with thee: be not dismayed; for I am thy God: I will strengthen thee; yea, I will help thee; yea, I will uphold thee with the right hand of my righteousness.
Isaiah 41:10 (King James Version)

Naomi Byler stood over the single bed in the second bedroom of the *daadi haus*. Lying on the orange, white, and blue quilt was a folded piece of paper. She stared at it for a long moment before picking it up.

Dear Naomi...

She sank to the bed, and her hands trembled as she continued reading.

I can't begin to explain what these last five days have meant to me. Being here, your very first Bed and Breakfast guest, getting to know you and your precious children—all of it has been a wonder. My life in Texas is hectic at best, frantic at worst. The deadlines for a journalist come hard and fast. But this assignment was different.

I don't say these things to garner your sympathy, only to try and explain what staying here has meant...

With a quick move, Naomi refolded the paper and stood. *No.* She didn't have time to read the letter right then. Her cheeks burned at the thought, and she knew she was deceiving herself. She had time. Of course, she had time.

But she wanted to avoid the confusing rush of feelings his words brought forth. Resolutely, she shoved the letter in her pocket and began to strip the bed. The sheets and pillowcase would be washed on Monday, along with the rest of the laundry. He would have left a dirty towel, too. She let the sheets fall onto the braided rug and folded the quilt at the end of the bed. No need to strip the other mattress. Justin Moore had come alone.

She moved into the bathroom and saw his towel hanging neatly over the bar. She pulled it loose, noting it was still damp. She moved back to the bedroom and dropped it on top of the sheets. Then she moved about the small *daadi haus*, dusting every surface with an old dishtowel. After that, she swept through all the rooms, whether Mr. Moore would have used them or not. Truth be told, the *daadi haus* wasn't large and giving it a thorough cleaning never took long.

All that was left was to wash down the tub and clean the toilet. Ten minutes tops. But it took her twelve minutes before she gathered up the laundry, glanced around the house one last time, and left. Outside, she nudged one of the porch rockers with her foot, lining it up precisely with the second rocker. While she had been busy inside, it had begun to sprinkle. She dashed out into it, feeling the light drops of moisture ping on her forehead. Good thing it wasn't Monday or the laundry would get a second washing with the rain.

She pushed through the side door of the big house and put the laundry into a basket in the washroom.

"*Mamm!*" called her daughter Katy from the kitchen. "Would you come here?"

Naomi went into the kitchen and saw Katy with her hands in a large glass bowl, pressing bits of dough together.

"What are you making?"

"Pie," Katy said simply. At eleven years old, the girl had a surprising knack for cooking and baking. "I can't find the rolling pin."

"Isn't it in the lower cupboard where it belongs?" Naomi moved to the cupboard. She pulled open the door and saw the rolling pin's spot was empty. She stood and put her hands on her hips. "Now, where did it go?"

Katy frowned. "I need it right now."

"I can see that." Naomi glanced around the kitchen, seeing nothing out of place.

"I bet Ben took it."

"What would your brother want with a rolling pin?" Naomi asked with a smile. "That boy doesn't cook."

"Who knows what he's up to?"

Naomi peered through the kitchen window scanning the front yard for her five-year-old son. "I don't see him. Put the crust dough in the refrigerator. It'll roll better chilled anyway."

"But I wanted to have the pie for supper."

Naomi stepped to her daughter and gave her shoulder a squeeze. "Don't fret. I'll find the rolling pin."

She was glad to go back outside, even in the rain. A strange restlessness moved through her, and she pushed down a sudden urge to run. Where to? She had no idea. What was the matter with her that day? She should be excited. The bishop had approved her request to open a Bed and Breakfast, and she'd made five hundred dollars with her first paying customer.

She should feel joy. And gratitude. And an eagerness to continue developing her new business.

Instead, she felt depression weigh down her shoulders and seep into her heart. *Isaac. If he were still alive, what would he think of this new development?* Would her late husband be happy for her? She shivered slightly as the rain gathered on her face and dripped down her neck. No. He wouldn't. He wouldn't want her attention split from the children and her household chores.

I have no choice, she said to herself, and in a way, to him. Leasing the farmland brought in just enough to cover the mortgage but not enough to live on. She *had* to earn more money.

She stood under the sweeping elm tree in the front yard and leaned against the bark, taking a moment out of the rain. She spotted Zachariah King out in her fields working. Even from such a distance, he cut a fine figure, muscular and sturdy. He was one of the steadiest people she knew, and she was grateful that he wanted to lease her land. It was strange— she really didn't know that much about him, but he was on her property nearly every day. Not that he spoke with her much. He was a quiet man, despite the amount of laughter she heard when he was with Ben.

A few days before, the two of them had gone frog hunting through the trees in the thicket down the road. Ben had come back splattered in dirt and all smiles. They'd located more than a few tree frogs, and Ben had gleefully announced that he was covered in frog germs. After a quick wash-up and a change of clothes, he was still recounting his adventure with excitement. When Naomi tucked him in after Bible reading that night, the last words on his lips were, "Mr. Zach knows where to find all the frogs..."

"*Mamm!*" Ben stood just inside the door of the barn and waved at her wildly.

"Benjamin!" Naomi hollered back. "I've been looking for you!"

She ran across the yard, her bare feet slipping in patches of mud. She dashed into the barn and wiped her forehead. "Do you have the rolling pin?"

Ben's face turned red. "Uh oh."

"Benjamin Byler! What were you thinking? Katy's in need of it." Naomi shook her head, suppressing a smile. "Where is it?"

"But *Mamm*, I needed it, too." Ben walked to the front corner of the barn. There he'd laid a scrap of plywood. On top of the wood was a pile of grain with the rolling pin sitting beside it.

"What the world are you doing?"

"I was thinking that I could set up a place to feed the frogs. But then I thought maybe the grain was too big or rough for 'em to swallow. So I'm smooshing it with the rolling pin."

Naomi looked down at her son's efforts and bit back a chuckle. "Benjamin, I'm thinking frogs don't eat grain."

"Horses do."

"*Jah*. But frogs don't. They eat flies and such."

Ben puckered his lips into a pout. "So I done this for nothin'?"

"You did it for nothing." Naomi bent down and retrieved the dusty rolling pin. "I think Mr. King needs to give you some more frog lessons."

"Can he come for supper then?" Ben asked, his face alight.

Naomi sighed. "I'm sure he's busy. He has his own family."

As she said it, she realized again how little she knew of Mr. King's family. She did know he wasn't married, which in itself was curious. Not many men in their late twenties or early thirties were still single in the district. Having been in Hollybrook for barely a year meant Naomi didn't know his history, unlike the rest of the folks around, who seemed to know absolutely everything about everyone, even down to the very hairs on their heads.

"Can I ask him?"

Since the accident that had killed her husband and her parents, Naomi hadn't seen much enthusiasm on Ben's face. Truth be told, she didn't want to invite Zach for supper. Somehow, it didn't seem appropriate. Plus, the man had been acting a bit odd of late. The other day, she'd wondered if he was jealous of her *Englisch* guest. But now, looking at her son's face, she was loath to squash his animation.

"Fine. But don't be surprised when he tells you no," she said, leaving the barn with the rolling pin in hand.

~

Zachariah King said yes. Naomi had to scramble to set another plate when she saw him coming through the field with Ben jumping about at his side. She shook her head, realizing that Zach had probably only agreed so as not to dampen Ben's spirits. So she and Zach had that in common then.

"Why's Mr. Zach coming to dinner?" Katy asked when Naomi told her.

"Because he's Ben's friend, and Ben wanted to invite him."

"Kind of old to be Ben's friend, don't you think?" Katy said, never at a loss to offer her judgment on a situation.

"Never you mind, daughter. Just get out another glass and utensils."

"*Mamm*!" Ben's voice echoed through the house. "He's staying!"

Naomi went to greet them as they came in through the side door. "Mr. King, how nice of you to join us."

He nodded and gave her a smile. He looked a bit embarrassed, and she wondered whether he was recalling his behavior of the other day. "I hope it's all right. Ben told me that you said it was fine."

"Ben was right. It *is* fine. Feel free to wash up. Supper's almost on the table." She scurried off, giving him time to clean up. She was surprised at her own nervousness. But then even before Zach's dislike of the *Englischer*, Naomi had often felt unsettled around him. She supposed it was because he always seemed ill at ease around her.

Katy's cherry pie had been done for a few hours, so its sweet smell had long since faded. Now the aroma of meatloaf and potatoes filled the house. Katy scooped the potatoes into a serving bowl while Naomi took the meatloaf from the oven.

"I'm mighty glad you baked a pie today. I'm sure Mr. King will find it tasty."

Katy gave a small smile, but Naomi could see the pride on her face. Inwardly, she sighed in relief. Perhaps Katy wouldn't be sour during supper after all.

"Someday, you're going to have a pie business," Naomi predicted. "Actually, your pies will probably bring guests to our Bed and Breakfast."

"You're really going to do it, then?"

"Yes, Katy girl, we're really going to do it." A flash of trepidation swept through her at her own conviction. But it would be all right. The Bed and Breakfast would work out. *Of course, it would.*

They carried the food out to the table. Zach and Ben were already there, freshly washed up. Zach had taken the spot at the end of the table where Isaac used to sit when he and her parents were still alive. Zach was a bigger man than her husband had been, and he looked downright overpowering at the end of the table. His shoulders were wide, and he carried a determination with him that seemed to fill the room. But right then, Naomi saw him fidget with the edges of his napkin as he placed it in his lap.

"Can Mr. Zach lead the prayer?" Ben asked, giving an appreciative glance to his friend.

Naomi's breath froze in her throat. *Zach lead the silent prayer?* She shifted in her chair. That seemed entirely too intimate and too familiar.

Zach reached over to where Ben perched on the long wooden bench. "*Nee,* Ben. That's for your *mamm* to do. I'm just a guest."

Naomi gazed at him. Zach gave her a steady look, and his eyes were thick with what looked like admiration and understanding. She gulped

71

and bent her head for prayer. Her mind fumbled to form her silent words to God, but Zach's presence had totally thrown her for a loop. And just what *was* that look he'd given her? Almost as if he could see right through her, into her very soul. Her chest constricted.

Focus, Naomi, focus.

But she couldn't. The weight of missing Isaac had settled into her heart, and she felt powerless against it. It sat in her like a rock. She squeezed her eyes more tightly, willing the tears to stay away. The seconds ticked by as she struggled to control her grief.

Too much time had passed. She cleared her throat, and everyone opened their eyes. Naomi gave a feeble smile, trying her best to mask her pain. Neither Katy nor Ben seemed to notice. but Zach's face became shadowed, and he looked directly at her until she averted her eyes.

It was obvious he knew how she suffered. She should feel comforted that someone could sense her pain, but she didn't. She felt flustered and on edge.

Why had Zach agreed to supper anyway? He leased her land. Period. If he hadn't been sitting there, she would have made it through dinner just fine. Yet even as she thought such things, she knew it was futile. Zach wasn't the cause of her overwhelming sadness.

She nodded at Katy. "Start the potatoes around, would you?"

Katy grabbed up the bowl and handed it to Zach. Ben took a drink of milk, leaving a white moustache on his upper lip. Katy giggled. "Wipe your mouth, Ben. You look like an old man!"

Ben turned his head about with a silly look on his face. "Do I look like a bishop?" He became stern and eagle-eyed. Then he laughed, and Katy joined in.

"Children!" Naomi scolded, jumping into their conversation with relief. "Be respectful, now." Bless the children for providing a distraction.

Zach smiled as he helped himself to a huge portion of potatoes. Naomi began to eat, working to swallow past the lump in her throat. She rested her left hand in her lap and heard the faint crinkle of the letter she'd pushed into her pocket earlier. *Justin's letter. The Englischer.* What would Zachariah think if he knew she had a letter from Justin Moore in her pocket? He wouldn't like it. He wouldn't like it at all.

She would finish reading it that evening in the privacy of her own room. A spark of unwelcome anticipation ran through her. Justin had eaten at that very table only this morning. It was strange to conceive it. But now he was gone, and she would never see him again.

As she took a drink of milk, she realized she would miss him. She shook her head and frowned. Whoever heard of missing a person they'd only known for five days? *Ridiculous.*

After eating two helpings of food, Zach scooted his chair back. "I need to be heading home," he said. "Thank you for the meal."

"But my pie!" Katy said. "I made a cherry pie."

Zach's eyebrows rose. "Did you now?"

Katy nodded.

"Well, I can't be missing that, then, can I?"

Katy jumped up and ran into the kitchen, returning with her cherry pie. "Should I bring in the pie plates?"

"I can use this plate," Zach said. "No need to be washing extra dishes."

Katy glanced at her mother, and Naomi nodded. Katy picked up her butter knife and began to cut the pie into six pieces. Then she walked around the table, serving each of them.

"Any ice cream?" Ben asked.

"*Nee.* We ate it all," Naomi responded.

"You mean Mr. Justin ate it all!" Ben said with a laugh.

"*Jah.* He surely did like ice cream." Naomi felt her cheeks flush. She blinked rapidly and quickly took a bite of pie. "Delicious, Katy. Once again."

Naomi felt Zach studying her. He hadn't been happy that Justin Moore, an *Englischer,* had been her very first boarder. He'd made that clear with his dour presence every time Naomi turned around. And now, he was making it even clearer with his smoldering eyes. She bristled under his gaze and purposefully looked away.

Thankfully, the children chattered through the dessert, relieving Naomi of any need to converse, and then it really was time for Zachariah to leave. Naomi got up to see him to the door, as was her duty as the hostess.

Zach paused with his hand on the doorknob and gazed down at her. "Thank you for the meal," he said, his voice low and resonant. "It was mighty good."

"I'm glad you liked it." The words came stilted from her lips.

Zach stepped outside. "I noticed a patch on the east side of your barn roof where the shingles are loose, and some of them are missing. It looks about to leak."

Naomi groaned inwardly. She had no money for repairs.

"Wait," he said, noting her obvious reaction. "I'm only telling you because you might wonder why I was climbing about on your roof. I'll be fixing it come tomorrow."

"*Nee!*" Naomi reacted. "You lease the land. That surely doesn't include fixing my barn roof."

Zach was still for a long moment. Then he spoke, and his words were slow and sure. "You're living in Hollybrook now. That's what we do."

Naomi closed her mouth, ashamed at her outburst. She remembered all the times in the past, back in Pennsylvania, when her husband and father had joined a group of Amish farmers to help Widow Maeve Bowman. Not just her, either, but the other widows. One time, they completely re-roofed Widow Parkin's house after a particularly windy spring.

So that was it. *She* was the widow now. *She* was the one who would receive help. She blanched, dismayed to her core to be in such a position.

"I don't have any shingles."

"I do," he said. He touched her wrist, and the very air around them became electrified. Her throat went dry, and she worked to swallow. *When did Zachariah become so disturbing?* She blinked up at him. His eyes were dark and unfathomable as he dropped his hand to his side. He gave her one long last look and then went down the steps and walked away.

She turned abruptly and hurried back inside. The day couldn't get over soon enough for her. She went back to the dining area and saw that the table had been cleared. In the kitchen, Katy was running the dish water.

"I'll take over from here," Naomi said. "Thank you for all your help. Why not go read a story to your brother? It'll be time for bed soon."

"But *Mamm*, it's not even eight o'clock yet."

Naomi blew out her breath. "It'll be time for bed soon," she repeated.

Chapter Two

❧

Thankfully, the children turned in without grumbles. Naomi simply couldn't abide one more hour of anything but solitude. She promised herself that she'd make it up to them the next day and allow them an extra half hour of play outside after supper.

The downstairs echoed its emptiness as Naomi walked through the rooms, adjusting the open windows and straightening odds and ends. The cool wooden floors felt refreshing on her feet, and she began to relax. The sun was sinking, and the shadows through the rooms deepened. She should light a lantern, but she resisted, instead enjoying the peaceful settling of the darkness. The breeze flowing through the windows was humid and heavy, and she smelled the fragrance of the growing plants outside. She could almost sense their developing ripeness, knowing that before long, canning season would be upon her. Harvest was always a frantic and an exciting time. Putting up all that food, feeling its richness, and knowing it was going to take the family through the winter, made a person safe and content.

Naomi had always enjoyed the changing seasons and the unique blessings and tasks that came with every shift of the earth. She stepped outside on the front porch and sank into one of the rockers. Would she be able to handle her Bed and Breakfast plus all the canning that year? Katy would be a big help, but she was only a child. Perhaps, Naomi and her friend Mary could do their canning together. Sometimes Amish women put up fruit and vegetables together, but having been in the district a limited time, Naomi wasn't sure about the women in Hollybrook. Besides, she'd never had the need as she'd always canned with her mother. But Mary would know, and Naomi decided to ask her friend about it soon.

Naomi's hand went to her pocket, and she felt the crunch of Justin's letters beneath her fingers. It was time. She pulled the letter out and unfolded it. She held it close to her face, but in the growing darkness, she couldn't make out Justin's words. She reached over to the small table beside her, found the matches, and lit the lantern there, carefully replacing the chimney.

She reread the first part of the letter. Then she focused on the last half.

I don't say these things to garner your sympathy, only to try and explain what staying here has meant to me. I love the quiet rhythm of your life. I love how you live so in tune with the earth and nature. Many people think everyone in Texas lives on a ranch. I can assure you—that isn't true. I live smack in the middle of the city, where things are fast and hectic and impersonal.

Ha! My mother always told me I was born in the wrong place. It used to annoy me, but I see the wisdom of her observation now. It really became pointed while staying with you at your Bed and Breakfast.

And to think that I gathered eggs! From real live hens. A highpoint in my life to be sure.

I do hope that you won't forget me, Naomi Byler. I hope we can continue to be friends. I can call you my friend, can't I?

Naomi leaned back against the chair and let out her breath. Was she his friend? She supposed so. And no, he needn't worry, she wasn't likely to forget him. She smiled, remembering how he could hardly fit his long legs beneath the dining table. Ben had to scoot the bench back before Justin could squeeze in. And she wouldn't soon forget the look of delight on his face when he found the eggs in the nesting boxes.

Naomi focused back on the letter.

My work takes me all over the United States. I can only hope that I'll get another writing assignment in Indiana. If I do, I hope you'll welcome me again at Byler's Bed and Breakfast. I'm smiling at you now, in case you don't know it.

Well, I suppose I need to close this letter. Think of me when I'm gone, Naomi. As I'll think of you.

With great esteem,

Justin Moore

He had added his mailing address at the end of his letter. She frowned and pressed her lips together. Did he expect her to write him back? She couldn't do that. It would be highly unseemly, plus nonsensical. What would be the point?

She folded the letter and pressed it back into her pocket.

The lantern had drawn all the nearby moths and other flying critters from the night. They circled and pinged against the glass chimney. Naomi swatted about herself and then stood. Snuffing out the flame, she went inside. It was time for bed.

Naomi sat at her husband's heavy desk and studied the ledger books. Figuring and refiguring her finances had become a necessary evil every morning. She cringed at the figures before her now. The money she'd received for boarding Justin was a big help, but it wasn't enough. Her idea of a Bed and Breakfast would do her no good without paying customers. She'd been working on a sign to hang out by the road, but it looked crude. She was no artist. And who would want to stay at a place with such an ugly sign?

Perhaps she could get someone to make one for her—which of course would mean more money that she didn't have.

Ben tumbled into the front room, wiping sleep from his eyes. "I'm hungry," he grumped.

Naomi stood. "Of course, you are. Come on, breakfast is ready." She bustled into the kitchen and grabbed a hot pad. She pulled open the oven door and removed a platter of steaming hotcakes.

"Yum! Can we have syrup, too?" Ben asked, his mood vastly improved.

"It's on the table." The two went to the dining table where Katy was already seated, everything ready.

"Katy, how would you like to help me with the Bed and Breakfast sign after we eat?" Naomi asked.

"We're making a sign?" Ben piped up.

"We need to let people know we're open for business," Naomi explained, realizing that she had to step into a business owner role.

"I'll help," Katy said.

Naomi smiled at her and reached over to pat her hand. "I don't know what I'd do without you, Katy girl," she said. "Shall we pray?"

After the kitchen was clean and the barn chores were finished, Naomi and Katy dragged out the large board Naomi had been working on. She'd taken some left-over paint and had tried to make a nice border around the edges. Unfortunately, Naomi's plan for a colorful, yet professional looking design left much to be desired.

"*Mamm*, it looks like a garden snake winding around the board," Katy said, standing with her legs apart, gazing at it.

Naomi burst out laughing. "You're right! I knew it was horrid, but I didn't know why. A snake!"

"Maybe the guests will think they'll have snakes in their beds." Katy giggled.

"*Jah*, and that we serve fried snake for supper."

"And we have a snake museum in our barn!" Katy grinned at her own joke.

Naomi shook her head and continued to chuckle. "Aw, Katy. I'm not good at this."

Katy tipped her head and studied the sign further. "Well, maybe we could make it into a vine with flowers."

Naomi considered that. "Do you want to give it a try? Look, I have all these bits of left-over paint. Nothing really colorful, though. The flowers are going to be drab."

"Where's the paintbrush?"

Naomi hurried back into the barn to fetch it. "Here you go. What can I do to help?"

Katy started giggling again. "*Mamm*, you've helped enough."

"Now, if the sign was on a quilt, I'd have done just fine," Naomi defended herself with a smile.

"Too bad we can't hang a quilt. It'd look so nice."

"The weather would destroy it."

Katy nodded. "*Jah*, it would."

A loud bang came from the top of the barn and both Naomi and Katy jumped and looked up.

"What was that?" Katy asked.

Then Naomi remembered. "I'm thinking it's Zach. He told me he was going to work on the barn roof today."

"What's wrong with it?"

"He said a part of it was about to leak." Naomi continued gazing up as she began moving around the barn, trying to locate Zach on the roof. Katy followed her. When they rounded the last corner, Naomi saw him. He was on his knees, nailing new shingles onto a darkened patch of roof.

He spotted her looking at him. "*Gut* morning, Naomi,. And Katy," he called down.

"*Gut* morning. Do you need anything?"

The brim of his hat shadowed his face. She couldn't see his features well, but she clearly saw his wide smile. "I'm fine," he said, pounding in another nail.

"All right, then. Thank you, Zach. Truly." She left him to it, and she and Katy returned to their sign project.

"Here's a stick to stir the paint," Naomi said, handing Katy a smooth branch. "Some of the colors might be okay because I stirred them yesterday. Some of this paint is ancient. Left behind by the previous owner, I suppose."

The two of them got to work. Naomi let Katy do the painting, but in all honesty, the sign still looked amateurish at best. Katy sank onto the ground. "*Mamm*, it's awful."

Naomi joined her on the grass. "It's not so bad."

But it was.

"The letters look like big blobs. The paintbrush is too fat. It's ugly, *Mamm*. For sure and for certain."

Naomi sighed. "It's the best we've got, so we don't have much choice. Perhaps in the future, we can have one specially made."

"Sorry it's so bad," Katy said, a dejected look on her face.

"No need to be sorry." Naomi patted her daughter on her back. "It's fine for now. We just have to nail it onto a post and put it at the end of the drive."

Ben came skipping from around the barn. "Can I go up on the roof and help Mr. Zach?" he asked.

Naomi frowned. "*Nee*. The roof's no place for a five-year-old."

"But I'm big now. You always tell me so."

Naomi gazed at his stubborn expression, and her heart softened. "You are big," she said with more gentleness. "But what would I do if you fell off the roof? Hmm? Who would help me with all the barn chores then?"

Ben looked as if he was considering this. His face brightened. "Then, can I help you with that?" He pointed to the sign.

"You sure can," Naomi said, relieved he'd given up the roof idea. "We need a long wooden post to nail this sign on."

"I know where one is," Ben cried, taking off in the direction of the chicken coop.

Within minutes, he was back, dragging a dirty post behind him and leaving a trail of smashed grass. "Here you go, *Mamm*."

"Where did you find that? It's quite perfect."

"Behind the coop. I spotted it a long time ago."

"Good for you, Ben. Can you fetch Katy and me a hammer and some nails?"

"Zach's using the hammer."

"We have more than one. Look on the tool shelf in the barn."

He was off, returning in two minutes with a hammer and a fistful of nails.

"Wait a minute, *Mamm*," Katy said. She bent over with the paintbrush and put another petal on a white flower. "Okay. That's better."

Ben and Katy held the sign over the post, while Naomi attempted to nail it down.

"Don't smear the paint!" Naomi warned, two nails sticking out of her mouth. She focused on her target and gave another swing with the hammer. The nail shot out, flying across the grass.

Naomi frowned, her brow wrinkling in concentration. She pulled another nail from her mouth and held it over the sign. Another swing. This time the nail went partway in and folded over to the side.

"You're no good at this," Ben observed.

Naomi sank onto her haunches. "I can see that, Ben."

"Let me try."

"*Nee.* I'm going to try again," she muttered.

"Need some help?"

Naomi looked up to see Zach standing a few yards away. His lips were pressed together, and Naomi could clearly see that he was biting back a smile.

"Mr. Zach!" Ben exclaimed, jumping up and letting the sign fall to the side. "*Mamm* ain't no good at all with a hammer."

Zachariah stepped closer, looking down at the sign. "Hmm." He gazed at Katy. "How are you this morning, Katy?"

"Fine." She grimaced. "The sign's ugly, but we did the best we could."

He squinted again at the sign. "*Nee,* it's not ugly."

"But it is," Katy insisted. "Someday, we're going to get us a proper sign."

Zachariah stood next to where Naomi squatted on the ground. She was completely aware of his nearness, and her heart beat faster. More and more she noted her reaction to his proximity, and she couldn't say she was pleased about it. She had no business being so interested in the comings and goings of Zachariah King.

She remembered that her friend Mary had offered to tell her Zach's story, whatever that might be. Naomi hadn't taken her up on the offer yet, but right then she decided she would do so. And right soon, if the occasion presented itself.

Zachariah got down on one knee beside her and took the hammer from her hand. She could see he was about to reach for the remaining nail which was between her lips. Quickly, she fumbled for it, pulling it out and handing it to him.

He held the nail against the bottom of the sign.

"Paint's still wet," Katy warned.

With a swift swing, the nail went successfully through the sign and into the pole. Ben let out a cheer. "See *Mamm*! Mr. Zach can do anything!"

Zach flushed at that and kept his eyes on the sign. "I need one more nail."

Ben scurried to the barn to get him one. "Here, you go," he said upon returning.

With another swing of the hammer, the sign was secure. Zach stood, pulling up the sign with him.

"Where do you want it?" he asked Naomi, looking at her with blue eyes that shone like cobalt.

She stepped back and swallowed. "Please don't worry yourself," she said, reaching to take the sign from him. "The children and I can take it from here."

He hesitated, not loosening his grip on the post. "It's no bother." His voice was low and thick with meaning.

Again, she wondered if he was somehow trying to announce his interest, stake his claim so to speak. She had wondered it the night he'd stopped in during the supper hour, when Justin Moore was staying. Now, she wondered it again.

But before she could determine anything, he let go of the post and nodded at her. "There you are then." And with that, he turned and walked back around the barn.

"Thank you," she called after him. Before Ben could urge him back, she smiled at her children. "Shall we go dig a hole?"

Ben grinned and ran toward the barn. "I'm gettin' the shovel!" he called over his shoulder.

They found a nice smooth spot at the base of their drive, and Naomi let Ben dig the first few shovelfuls. It was hard-going, though, and Katy took over. After she'd dug a few shovelfuls full of rocks mixed with the dirt, she handed the shovel to Naomi.

"How deep does it got to be?" Ben asked.

"Deep enough so it doesn't fall over in the first wind."

Katy scowled. "I think we need some cement."

Naomi stood straight and regarded her daughter. "You're probably right, but we'll try it this way first." She dug further and then picked up the sign.

"I'll hold it for you, *Mamm*," Ben offered, dragging the sign into the hole and standing it up straight.

"Thank you, son." Naomi shoveled loose dirt and rocks around the post. Katy stomped it down hard. Naomi dropped the shovel and joined her in jumping up and down on the dirt. She looked at Katy and started to laugh.

"Is this what the *Englisch* call dancing?" she asked.

Katy grinned. "I don't think so."

Naomi grabbed her hands around the sign, and they began circling it, stomping and laughing. Ben let go of the post and joined them. They went round and round until Naomi was dizzy.

"Stop!" she cried holding up her hand. "I'm going to fall over!"

"This is fun," Ben said, grabbing Naomi around the waist.

"*Jah*, it is." Naomi backed up a few paces and observed the sign.

Byler's Bed & Breakfast.

"It doesn't look so bad," Katy said.

"I think it looks right fine," Naomi assured her. "Thank you, children, for your help. Now, let's hope we get some business."

They walked back to the barn, with Ben dragging the shovel behind him.

Chapter Three

Naomi stood at the clothesline, hanging up the sheets from the *daadi haus*. When she hung the towel that Justin had used, her mind went to the letter she'd tucked safely away in her top drawer under her neatly organized clothes. Her thoughts circled the return address he'd put at the bottom of the page. Did he truly expect her to write back?

She'd asked herself the question a hundred times. Part of her wanted to. In fact, it would be right nice to have a pen pal of sorts. She could tell him about the bishop's approval and the new sign on the road. She could tell him that she was thinking about getting a cell phone so that potential guests could contact her.

But why would Justin Moore be interested in such things? And why would she tell him such things in the first place?

Annoyed with herself, she fished another towel out of the basket and hung it up. A faint breeze rippled the fabric. If that kept up, it wouldn't take long for the clothes to dry. She heard a horse approach, and she turned around in time to see Mary coming up the drive in her pony cart.

Naomi left her laundry basket where it sat and hurried to meet her friend.

"Mary! How nice of you to come. How are your boys getting along?"

Mary climbed from her cart and threw the reins around the hitching post. "*Ach*! Back to themselves, they are. Now Betty is sick. Dear Lord, I knew it was coming." She patted her chest. "But I'm fit as a fiddle, make no mistake."

"Can you sit awhile?"

"Would like to," Mary answered. "I came to give you the rest of the pie money. Thank you again for helping me out by baking those pies for my road stand." She dug in her apron and pulled out a handful of cash. "I'm sorry I didn't get this to you sooner."

Naomi took the money. "No need to be sorry. I was grateful for the opportunity."

"You made one hundred and fifty dollars, plus whatever you got for that first pie you sold."

"This is a big help, Mary. Thank you."

The two women climbed the steps to the porch and sat in the rockers. Mary was there only a minute before Naomi sprang back up. "*Ach*, where are my manners? Would you like some lemonade? It's already quite hot out."

Mary nodded, rocking slowly. "Sounds nice."

Naomi scurried inside to get two glasses of lemonade. When she returned, Mary's eyes were closed, and she was no longer rocking. Had the woman fallen asleep? Naomi smiled and sat quietly beside her.

"I ain't sleepin' if that's what you think," Mary murmured.

"You go right ahead and sleep if you want to."

Mary's brown eyes popped open. "I'm fine. A little catnap does wonders."

Naomi laughed. "Well, that catnap was about four minutes long."

Mary shrugged. "T'was enough."

The two women sipped their drinks and sat in companionable silence until Naomi remembered her decision regarding Zachariah's story. "You were going to tell me about Zachariah King," she said, questioning if such talk would classify as gossip. She chewed the inside of her lip, wondering if she was displeasing God.

"That I was," Mary said, sitting up straighter. "Such a nice man, Zachariah." She looked at Naomi and raised her right brow. "Any interest there?"

Naomi blushed. Back in Pennsylvania where Naomi was from, courting and love interests were not discussed. Were things different in Hollybrook?

Mary slapped her own leg and let out a chuckle. "I can see by your face that you aren't going to divulge a thing. No matter. You're part of the district now and should know about the people."

Naomi nodded, relieved Mary wasn't going to push the matter. Truth was, Naomi had no idea whether there was interest there. Her heart beat harder when Zach was around, but she was pretty sure it was because the man made her nervous. He certainly seemed ill at ease around her. She stopped rocking, and her thoughts sharpened. Until the last day or two. Zach hadn't seemed ill at ease in the least when he'd fixed her roof or when he'd helped with the sign.

"Naomi?" Mary questioned.

Naomi gave a start. "What? Oh, I'm sorry. What were you saying?"

"You have a new sign I see."

"*Jah*. It's crude, but it'll do."

"I hear Jacob Westwork is a master at working with wood. He could make you one."

Naomi thought about the money she'd just gotten from Mary and knew it wouldn't be enough. "Perhaps. But in the meantime, it's acceptable, don't you think?"

Mary shrugged. "Certainly. But if you change your mind, I'll put in a word."

Naomi took another sip of lemonade. "Thank you."

"Now, about Zachariah." Mary's eyes got a faraway look in them. "He was a bit younger than me in school. A bright boy, I remember that. But quiet. Never said much. Anyway, he was the youngest of a parcel of children. Not coddled, mind you. Truth be told, I think his mother was downright exhausted when he came along. Pretty much raised himself." She laughed.

Naomi nodded, visualizing a young Zach keeping to himself amidst a huge family. A ping of sadness ran through her; her own family would never be large, but she did have the two children, and she was grateful. She craned her neck and saw Ben and Katy playing on the tire swing out back. She'd wanted more than two children. In fact, she'd hoped to have another on the way by that summer. But now, with Isaac gone, she was relieved it hadn't happened. She was barely surviving with trying to take care of the children she did have. And Isaac would never have laid eyes on his third child.

"When Zach was a teen, he didn't really participate in his *rumspringa* time. He just kept working the farm with his *dat*. But he was sweet on Marcy Blaeckenship. That girl was something else! New to the district and full of spice, that one." Mary shook her head.

"Zach fell hard for her. Took her to Sunday youth singings a couple times. *Before* she began her *rumspringa*, that is."

Naomi leaned forward in her chair. She could tell where this was heading.

"Marcy went a bit crazy. She would disappear for days on end. Like I said, Zach was always a quiet sort, but when Marcy was gone, he wouldn't speak at all. At least in public. I can't vouch for him at home. When I'd see him at church, he was like a closed door."

Mary reached out and touched Naomi's arm. "It was the worry. He was worried sick for her. With cause, too, as it turned out."

"How sad," Naomi said, imagining how Zach must have felt.

"Marcy's parents were frantic. I know they went to the bishop for help, but there wasn't much to be done. Wait it out, I suppose. And pray. I think everyone in the district prayed for the girl. When she'd swoop back into Hollybrook, though, she'd make some of the people so upset."

Mary shook her head and sighed. "She flaunted herself, and it got so bad that folks were hiding their *kinner* when she'd come around." Mary rocked hard in her chair. "But Zach stayed true. I know he attempted to see her when she was here. Sometimes, she'd calm down, too. Put her Amish clothes back on. Attend a Sunday meeting here and there. She'd sit with the women, her back straight as a board. But there was something in her eyes, something wild and proud."

"What did Zachariah's parents say about it all?"

Mary sighed. "They wanted to send Zach off to relatives in Ohio, but he talked them out of it. I think he figured if he left, there would be no one to bring Marcy back to the church."

The two women fell silent. Naomi turned her head and gazed out into her fields. She couldn't see Zach, but she knew he was out there somewhere, working. "That's so sad. Whatever happened to her? To her family?"

Mary threw out her hand in a dismissive wave. "The whole family packed up and left. Just like that. It was too much to bear."

"And Marcy?"

"Who knows?" Mary clucked her tongue. "Although, Zach probably knows. Thing is, I believe they were engaged."

Naomi's brows shot up. "Really?"

"*Jah.* Pretty sure. Of course, we keep such news quiet around here—

despite my teasing you—but I think they were. No other reason for Zach to react in such a way."

"Maybe he loved her."

"He loved her all right." Mary grimaced. "The man's still single, ain't he?"

Naomi nodded, still grasping what the whole experience must have done to Zach.

"Never saw him interested in anyone since." Mary leaned close and laid her hand on Naomi's knee. "Till you, maybe."

Naomi jerked back against the rocker. "*Nee*. He's not interested in me."

"You sure about that, Naomi Byler? You sure?" Mary didn't wait for an answer. She set her empty glass on the small table by her chair and heaved herself to her feet. "I need to get back to my brood," she announced. "Been gone long enough. Thank you for the lemonade."

Naomi stood, blinking at the rapid end to the conversation.

Mary huffed down the steps, grabbed the reins, and climbed into the pony cart. "Mind my words, dear friend." She gave Naomi a smile and a nod before she slapped the reins on the pony and went on her way.

Naomi watched her leave. She ran her finger around the top rim of her glass, over and over, as her mind circled what she now knew. *Oh, Zachariah.* How he must have hurt. And it must have gone deep, or he would be married by now and have a passel of children. Absently, she set down her glass and walked back out to her laundry basket.

Was Zachariah interested in her? And why? She was nothing special. She bent down and grabbed a wadded-up sheet from the basket. She shook it out and flung it over the line, clipping it in place with three clothespins. A gust of wind blew the sheet back into her face, and she laughed as it softly whipped her cheeks.

She heard the crunch of gravel and a car motor behind her. She turned and saw a pale yellow pick-up truck approach her porch. She hurried to greet whomever it was.

A tired-looking woman, with graying brown hair rolled down her window. "Is this the Bed and Breakfast?" She pointed over her shoulder. "We saw the sign."

Excitement surged through Naomi. "It is. Would you like to stay?"

The woman let out a groan. "Thank God! We're so exhausted." She gestured with her thumb to the man driving. He looked older than she was; his hair had already turned completely white. "My dumb husband managed to get us lost about five times today so far. We're supposed to be miles closer to Chicago by now." She gave a disgruntled sigh.

"When are you going to let up?" the man interjected from the driver's seat. "This fine woman don't need to hear your griping and fussing."

The woman pursed her lips. Naomi stepped back, wondering what kind of guests these two would be. But she wasn't in a position to be picky, and they seemed safe enough.

"I need to explain something," Naomi said, putting on her friendliest smile. "This is a real Amish experience, so there isn't any electricity. However, there is a hot shower and good home-cooked meals."

"No Internet then?" the woman asked.

Naomi braced herself. "No."

"Good!" she exclaimed. "This guy sticks his face into his tablet, and I don't see a lick of him all evening long." She glared at her husband. "Hear that? Now we can have a proper conversation."

The man rolled his eyes, and Naomi felt pity for him. Who would want a conversation with her?

"How much a night?" the woman asked.

"One hundred dollars."

"And that includes some meals?"

"It does. I'll be serving supper at six."

The woman was already opening her door. When she stepped out,

Naomi was surprised at how short she was. Short or not, she slammed her door with enough force to shake the truck. "Get them bags, Harv," she ordered. She turned to Naomi. "Name's Clara. That there is Harv."

Naomi nodded. "Nice to meet you. Let me show you to your lodgings."

"Don't we stay in this here old house?" Clara asked, her eyes roaming over the place.

"*Nee*. You'll be staying in the *daadi haus* out back."

"The *what* house?"

"I'll show you." Naomi smiled and led the woman around the house. She heard the other truck door slam. She glanced over her shoulder and saw Harv lugging two bags and scrambling to catch up.

"Shall we wait for your husband?" Naomi asked.

Clara made a face. "I guess. Boy, has he slowed down in the last few years."

"I'm coming," Harv called out, huffing a bit.

When he caught up, Naomi took them up the steps and into the *daadi haus*. Clara looked about, her face lighting up. "Why, this is downright cozy." She walked to the lantern on the table. "We used to use lanterns just like this when we went camping. Remember that, Harv?"

Harv dropped both bags on the floor with a resounding thud. "Yes, Clara, I remember."

Naomi walked toward the bedroom and knew she had to make a quick decision. When Justin Moore had stayed, she'd put him in what used to be her children's room. She couldn't abide having him sleep in the same bed where she and Isaac had slept. It had seemed wrong, somehow. But now, with a couple, how could she offer them the room with the two single beds when there was a perfectly good room with a double bed.

She swallowed past the growing lump in her throat and resolutely directed them toward her former bedroom. She pushed open the door, and her breath caught as she once again looked at the familiar space. Images of Isaac filled her mind, but she stubbornly forged ahead. "Here is your room," she said, forcing a smile.

Clara looked about and cackled like one of the hens in the coop outside. "Oh, honey, don't you have a room with two beds? Harv and I don't sleep together."

Naomi's eyes widened, and she struggled not to show her relief. "I do. Right in here." She took them to her children's room. "There are two mighty comfortable beds right in here."

Clara plunked down on the bed closest the window. "I'll sleep here. Harv, you can take that one."

Harv nodded, his cheeks reddening.

Naomi had never seen a wife treat her husband with such disrespect. It was bordering the scandalous. Was this how *Englischers* related to one another in marriage? The closest thing she'd ever witnessed to this was back in Pennsylvania when Ona Helmuth had harshly scolded her husband in front of the whole district for forgetting to bring his tools to a barn raising. Everyone had looked away in shame. Such an uncomfortable feeling. Walter Helmuth's face had turned beet red, and he'd hustled her right back into their buggy and took off. When he'd returned to help, *with his tools*, Ona was nowhere in sight.

"So, dinner is at six?"

"*Jah*, supper is at six."

Clara patted the quilt she was sitting on. "Don't we have to sign some type of register or something?"

Naomi's mind whirled. She had no register. "*Jah*, of course," she said, "but you can sign it when you come in to eat." She figured she could use the back portion of her ledger book for a register. She grimaced. What else didn't she have in place for this new business?

"Thank you kindly, ma'am," Harv said. "We'll be on time to eat. Don't you worry."

Naomi smiled. "I'm not worried at all. Now, you have fresh towels in the bathroom. Let me know if you need anything else."

"Is it all right if I leave my truck where it is? Or do you want me to move it elsewhere?"

Naomi considered that. "It's fine for now. You're tired. Why not take a rest?"

He looked relieved. "Don't mind if I do."

"Now, Harv, don't sleep away the rest of the day," Clara said.

Naomi took her leave, shutting the screen door gently behind her. Land's sake, what must living with that woman be like? She grinned just thinking about it.

"What's so funny?"

She flinched and looked to her left, seeing Zachariah approach. "My guests. *Ach*, it's nothing."

"I saw the truck pull in. Made quite a cloud of dust."

"That it did." She gave a quick glance to her damp laundry, some still in the basket. "I hope it didn't dirty my laundry."

He fell into step beside her, and her mind returned to all she'd learned about him. He paused at the clothesline as if waiting for her to say something. She looked at him, but all she could think of was Marcy and how the girl had hurt him.

Zach's expression turned puzzled, and his eyes narrowed. "I saw Mary came by earlier. She been talking about me?"

Naomi flinched. Were her thoughts written so clearly on her face? "What do you mean?"

He shook his head. "Nothing. Just a look in your eyes."

She licked her lips, unaccustomed to such familiar talk with a man who wasn't family. She certainly wouldn't have expected such a discussion with Zachariah. Up until the previous week, he'd hardly said two words to her.

"*Jah*, Mary came by," she blurted and then clamped her mouth shut. What was she planning to say?

He nodded slowly, and a knowing came over his face. "So, she told you, then?"

Naomi took a deep breath but didn't respond. Zach continued to look at her, his clear blue eyes watching her, assessing her. Naomi's heart raced. She bent down to grab another piece of laundry. She put a couple clothespins in her mouth and set about her work, trying to pretend he wasn't there; trying to pretend that his presence wasn't filling the air around her.

It didn't work. His nearness was like a physical force, surrounding her, making it difficult to function properly. Finally, after clumsily clipping three of Ben's shirts to the line, she dared glance over at him. He met her gaze and said one word. "Marcy."

Naomi dropped her hands to her sides. "*Jah*."

With a sharp inhale, he looked up at the sky for a moment then back to her. "If you'd lived here your whole life, you'd already know the story. So, I guess no harm done."

"I'm sorry, Zach."

"For what?"

"For the way Marcy treated you. For the way it all worked out."

His jaw tightened, and she wondered if she'd gone too far. "She's living in Cleveland now."

Naomi's eyes widened. "Cleveland?"

"She was in Chicago for a while, but she followed some guy to Cleveland."

"So, she's married? Has a family?"

He shook his head. "I don't know if she's married. She has two children, though."

Naomi reached out to touch his arm but thought better of it. "I'm sorry."

"She writes me. Not often. Maybe every year or two."

That was surprising news. Why would Marcy continue to write him unless ... unless, she was still in love with him. Was Marcy hoping for something further from Zach? And did Zach write her back? Naomi wanted to know so badly that she had to bite her lower lip to keep from asking. It wasn't her business. No matter how she looked at it; it wasn't her business at all.

Zach took a step closer, and her whole being seemed to be filled with waiting. His gaze was penetrating, and she found that she couldn't look away.

"*Mamm!*" Ben hollered from the front porch. "*Mamm*, Katy's wanting you!"

Naomi flinched and blinked rapidly. "All right!" she called back, her eyes still on Zach.

Zach stepped away and looked at the ground, but not before she saw a flush in his cheeks. "I need to go," she said. There was a quiver in her voice.

"Of course," he muttered. He ran his hands down his sides.

She hurried toward the porch, her heart still beating rapidly.

"Naomi?" Zach called after her.

She stopped and looked over her shoulder at him. He studied her face, the laundry fluttering in the breeze at his side. "I never write her back."

Naomi hesitated, feeling relief whoosh through her stomach. She gave him a slight nod and then disappeared inside the house, wondering why she should care so much.

Chapter Four

Katy helped immensely with getting supper on the table that evening for their guests. Naomi was pleased to note the happy way her daughter bustled about the kitchen. If Naomi didn't know better, she'd say Katy was downright giddy about cooking for company.

"What are they like, *Mamm*?" Katy asked as Naomi arranged raw vegetables on a platter.

"Hmm. Interesting," Naomi replied. "You'll see soon enough."

As soon as the words escaped her lips, she heard a commotion at the front door. She threw down her dishtowel and rushed to attend to her guests.

"Harv, for pity's sake, quit crowding me!" Clara fussed, as they both tumbled in the door.

"Good evening," Naomi said, opening the door even wider. "Come right in."

"I was trying, but this one," Clara jerked her head toward Harv, "wants to walk on my toes."

Harv rolled his eyes and smiled at Naomi. "You've got a beautiful place here."

Naomi returned his smile. "Thank you."

"My, what smells so good?" Clara walked past Naomi toward the dining area. When she caught sight the table, where Katy had already set out half the food, she gave an appreciative whistle. "This looks fit for a king!"

The woman climbed over the bench and tucked herself in. "Can't hardly wait to eat a real live Amish-cooked meal."

Harv followed Naomi. She offered him a seat at the end of the table, instead of next to his wife. Actually, Clara was sitting in Ben's spot, which Naomi was quite certain her son wouldn't like. Right then, Ben came skidding into the room, stopping short when he saw Clara.

"Ben," Naomi said, hurrying to him. She put her hands on his shoulder and squeezed. "I thought you could sit next to Katy this evening." She gave him a pointed look.

He peered around her at Clara, and Naomi saw his look of dismay. "All right, *Mamm.*"

When everyone got situated, Naomi spoke. "Shall we say the silent blessing?"

She wondered how Clara and Harv would react, but like her first guest Justin Moore, the two of them bowed their heads without a word. She sent up her prayer to God.

Gott, thank You for sending two more guests to us this night. Help them to be blessed and to rest well. Guide me as I tend to their needs. Thank You for my children and for the food You have given us. Amen.

Naomi cleared her throat and everyone looked up. "Katy, would you like to start the potatoes around?"

The meal went smoothly. Clara was so busy eating second and third helpings that she didn't have time to talk. Surprisingly, she barely said a word. As Naomi watched the woman eat, she began to wonder whether she should charge extra for meals. However, Harv didn't eat as much as Clara. All he had was one full plate and a generous helping of Katy's pie.

After finishing his food, Harv put down his fork, stood, and stretched. "Thank you, Ms. Byler. I think I'll turn in now."

"You're welcome. You know where the lanterns are, *jah?*"

"Yes, ma'am."

Clara dabbed at the corners of her mouth with her napkin. "It'll be just like camping again, won't it, Harv?" She extricated herself from the bench. She moved her head this way and that as if stretching her neck. "Driving for hours on end really does put an ol' crick in the neck, doesn't it?"

"I'm sure it must," Naomi replied.

"Let's leave these fine people alone now." Harv glanced at both Katy and Ben. "Nice to meet you young folks. We'll see you in the morning. Clara, you coming?" He looked at her expectantly.

Clara scowled but followed him to the door. "What time is breakfast?" she asked.

"I can serve it at seven-thirty, if that suits."

"That will be fine," Harv said before his wife could respond.

"I guess he's doing all the talking for me tonight," Clara said with a grunt.

As they went out the door, Naomi heard Clara scolding Harv about what a big mouth he had. Naomi shook her head. She would never get used to hearing a wife speak to her husband like that. Why, it would create total anarchy in the home. She snickered. She wished Isaac could be there to witness it. He'd be shocked beyond words.

Naomi saw her guests off after breakfast. Clara seemed quite excited about their stay, saying she would recommend Byler's Bed and Breakfast to all her friends. Naomi groaned inwardly. Would Clara's friends have the same sort of personality as Clara? And then she admonished herself. It wasn't her place to judge. Besides, the one hundred dollars she'd received didn't depend on personalities, now, did it?

During the early afternoon, Naomi took a break from her cleaning and walked out to the mailbox to fetch any letters that might have been delivered. Her eldest brother in Pennsylvania had taken to writing her nearly every week. Mostly to urge her return, but he often included a tidbit of news about the family. Naomi had gotten in the practice of skimming the first part of his letters where he chastised her for remaining in Indiana and focusing in on the news. She enjoyed hearing how the *kinner* were doing, and she liked hearing about the district happenings.

Naomi was grateful that her children never mentioned wanting to move back to Pennsylvania. She had thought they'd be yearning for their old home, but they hadn't said more than a word or two, causing her to think that her decision to stay put after the accident had been the right one.

She paused for a moment to look at her Bed and Breakfast sign before grabbing the mail. It was still standing upright, so evidently cement hadn't been necessary after all. Nestled there next to a young poplar tree didn't help the beauty of the sign's design, but even so, it had been effective, getting them guests. Still, someday, she'd like to have something nicer-looking. She opened the metal door of the mailbox and reached inside. There was only one letter, and when she pulled it out, she quickly saw it wasn't from her brother. When she noted the return address, her knees went weak, and she nearly stumbled right there on the road.

Texas!

Naomi only knew one person from Texas. *One.*

She stuffed the letter into her pocket and rushed back to the house.

Why was he writing her? And so soon? Had something happened? And if it had, why would he tell *her* about it?

She headed straight upstairs to her room, and sank onto her bed. Her hand shook as she retrieved the letter from her pocket. With a quick movement, she ripped it open. Her breathing turned shallow as she unfolded the paper and began to read.

Dear Naomi Byler,

You must think it odd to be receiving another letter from me so soon. You haven't responded to my first letter yet, but I felt the need to write again. I hope you'll forgive my eagerness.

Naomi took an unsteady breath and forced herself to calm down. There was no call for her to be so nervous about a letter. Nervous or ... *excited?* Which was it? She shuddered and focused again on Justin's words.

Upon my return to Texas, I plunged right into my work. As I told you before, life here is hectic, fast, and often impersonal. When I go home at night to my apartment, to my electricity, to my every convenience, I find my heart is still in Amish country. I find my thoughts are still on you. What is Naomi doing right now? I wonder. Is Ben finding any more frogs in the trees? Has Katy made more pies?

It's silly, really. I was there for a mere five days, but I can't shake it from my every waking thought. Soon, my boss will scold me for daydreaming! Ha!

Have you traveled much, Naomi? I wish you could see my home state. It's beautiful. And vast. The land varies from region to region. I've seen most every inch, what with growing up here and my journalism assignments. You would like the wide open spaces, I'm thinking. You would like the agriculture here. And the ranches. Ever been to a dude ranch? Ha! I imagine you haven't.

A dude ranch? Naomi had no idea what that was. Of course, she knew about ranches, but dudes? She squinted her eyes, pondering. Wasn't dude the *Englisch* word for a friend or a boy? If so, *dude ranch* didn't make much sense. She smiled and continued.

I'd love to take you to a dude ranch sometime. There's a fine one close to my city. Actually, they're scattered throughout the state. A good way to cash in on some major tourism dollars.

I hope you're having guests at your Bed and Breakfast now. Of course, it hasn't been so long since I left. You may not have gotten anyone yet. So am I your one and only so far?

Naomi blanched at his words. Her *one and only?* Uneasiness crept through her. Surely he didn't mean that the way it sounded. Was he becoming brazen with her? She dropped the letter onto her lap. Perhaps she shouldn't continue reading. She stood up and Justin's letter fluttered to the floor. It landed right-side up, and she stared at it. With a start, she realized she was still trying to read his words, but she couldn't from that distance.

She bent down and picked it up as guilt pinged through her mind. But in truth, it *was* a letter to her. She had an obligation to read it, didn't she?

Zach had read the letters that came from Marcy.

She didn't have to respond to Justin. Yet, he sure would be happy to know of her two guests. She sank back on the bed, and her hand trembled as she held the letter up once again.

I was thinking that perhaps I could help advertise your place. You mentioned the possibility of securing a phone for your business. Have you done that yet? Is it even allowed? If you had a phone, I could refer people to your number.

Please let me know. I would dearly love to be of assistance to you in any way I can. Well, I think this letter has been long enough. I find myself reluctant to stop writing, for this feels almost as if we're talking to one another.

A one-sided conversation to be sure!

If you can, please write me back.

Sincerely,

Justin Moore

He'd written his phone number across the bottom of the letter. Why, she couldn't call him even if she *did* have a phone. It would be completely frowned upon. More than that, it was forbidden. She folded his letter back up and stuck it in the envelope. She stood and walked to her dresser. Pulling open the top drawer, she felt under her clothing for his first letter. When her hand felt the edges of the paper, a tingling shot through her. She tucked the new letter under the old.

She pushed the drawer shut and went back to her bed to sit down. She glanced at her bedside table. She hadn't written in her journal for a day or two, and she should get caught up on it. She could take a few more moments to herself. The children were playing out back and most of the supper meal was to be left-overs from the day before. Lying back on her pillow, she stared up at the ceiling.

Was Justin Moore sweet on her? Katy had accused him of that very thing a few days ago. Not to his face, of course. She'd shot the words at Naomi. But why would he be sweet on her when he knew full well that nothing could come of it.

So why am I even thinking about it? And why does my heart beat faster when I think of him?

Naomi closed her eyes and forced herself to take slow even breaths. She lay motionless, but her mind whirled with troubling thoughts. She felt tears gather in her eyes and slip down her cheeks, but still, she didn't move.

If only Isaac was there. If only he hadn't died. If only...

She squeezed her eyes shut. No. God was sovereign. He was *not* to be questioned. A sudden image of Zachariah on her barn roof filled her mind. She saw him on his haunches, nailing the new shingles into place. She saw him look down at her and smile.

Now, her barn wouldn't leak, and the hay wouldn't mold.

She turned to her side and drew her knees to her chest. What an odd thing to come to mind right then. What an odd thing, indeed.

~

The following week saw no guests at Byler's Bed & Breakfast. Naomi walked out to the road each evening to make sure their sign was still in place.

"You have to advertise," Mary admonished her one morning. "Customers don't usually fall out of the sky."

Naomi looked at her friend. "Do you advertise? For your road stand?"

Mary laughed. "*Nee.* Don't have to." She shook her head. "I guess customers do fall from the sky."

Naomi sighed. Mary reached over and squeezed her arm. "Don't fret. It will happen. Things take time, you know."

"That I know," Naomi answered. Her mind flitted to her children and how long it had taken them to smile again. She still wondered about Katy. The girl turned sour so easily these days.

"I'm glad you stopped by to visit. You do know about the quilting frolic this Saturday, don't you?"

Naomi paced herself with Mary's short legs as they returned from the chicken coop with Mary's apron full of eggs.

"*Nee*, I didn't know. Can I bring the children?"

"Naomi Byler! Of course, bring the children. There will be a flock of them. Lois Schrock is hosting, and she always has a table of goodies for them. My young ones love going to her house. Some of the older girls like caring for the young ones, too. Your Katy might like that." She nudged Naomi. "The children are entertained so we women are left quite alone."

Naomi grinned and knew the Amish grapevine would be in full swing that day.

"I'd better be getting back," Naomi said. "Katy and Ben are weeding the garden, and they'll be wanting a snack right soon."

"Thank you again for taking the time to stop by," Mary said. "I'll see you Saturday around nine, then?"

"*Jah*, you'll see me Saturday."

Naomi hurried down Mary's drive out to the road. She'd walked that morning, feeling the need to clear her head with the bright sun and a leisurely pace. She'd been stewing of late, more than usual. Trusting the Lord God with her finances was becoming more and more difficult. She'd thought she had found the answer with the Bed and Breakfast, but without guests, it was not helping at all. Thank goodness she hadn't spent money on it yet. She'd been ready to get herself a cell phone, but she'd put it off. Now, she was glad she had.

Two sparrows chased each other in front of her, finally settling on a tree branch close to the road. She gazed at the two tiny creatures as they fluttered their wings and jerked their heads about.

"Looking for your next meal?" she asked them. "God speed to you."

As she neared her house, she was surprised to see a red car parked in front of the house. She increased her pace. Guests? Katy was standing on the porch, talking with two women. When Katy spotted her mother, she waved her over even though Naomi was already on her way.

"*Gut* afternoon," Naomi said with a wide smile. "Can we be helping you?"

The taller of the women turned to her. "We saw the sign. We'd like to stay the night." She tipped her neatly coifed head toward Katy. "Your daughter here says you have a vacancy."

Naomi gave Katy a grateful nod. "My daughter is correct. Will it just be the two of you? And how many nights would you like to stay?"

The short woman clapped her hands, and Naomi couldn't help but notice how the flesh of her arms flapped when she did so. "This is marvelous!" the woman exclaimed, her voice high and animated. "I've told my husband for years that I wanted to know more about the Amish." She leaned toward Naomi as if telling her a secret. "For *years*, mind you. He won't believe our luck!"

"Neither will mine," the tall woman said. "One night only. And yes, just the two of us. How much will this cost? And will we need to share a room?"

Naomi's mind flitted to her old bedroom, the one where no one had stayed as of yet. "*Nee*," she said, hiding her reluctance. "You can each have your own room. The cost is one hundred dollars, which includes meals if you choose. Please follow me."

The two women scurried to get their bags and followed Naomi. She'd left the windows open in the *daadi haus,* and it smelled fresh and sweet when they entered.

"I do need to explain that we have no electricity. This is an authentic experience," Naomi said, praying they wouldn't change their minds.

"No electricity?" the short woman said, stopping. A doubtful look crept over her face.

"Oh, for heaven's sake, Lynnette," scolded the taller. "You can live without your precious television shows for one night!"

Lynnette scowled. "And what about you, Nadine? What are you going to do when your tablet battery goes dead?"

Nadine huffed. "I'm *not* going to complain, that's what. Look, this is our chance. You going to spoil it because of no electricity?"

Naomi felt like an eavesdropper, standing there while they made up their minds.

Lynnette clucked her tongue and shook her head. "Of course, I'm not." She looked at Naomi. "Please forgive me. I'm an old fool. This is perfect."

The two women looked around the small house. Lynnette walked to the kitchen sink and peered out the window. "Is this one of those daddy houses?"

Naomi bit back her smile. "We call it a *daadi haus*. But, in a way, it is a daddy house."

"Shouldn't your elderly parents be living here?" she continued.

"Lynnette! You're being nosy." Nadine looked at Naomi. "You don't have to answer that. Honestly, how rude!"

"It's fine," Naomi said, realizing that she'd better get used to prying questions if she was going to host outsiders. "My parents are both deceased. The rest of my kin live in Pennsylvania."

"Then why'd you move to Indiana?"

"Lynnette! Stop harassing the poor woman." Nadine's small gray eyes settled on Naomi. "But really, why *did* you move here?"

Naomi swallowed. "My husband and father wanted to farm this land."

"Of course," Nadine responded. "Makes sense. How are they doing then? How does your father like it around here?"

"He was killed in a traffic accident." Naomi moved to the bedrooms. Enough was enough.

"Oh, honey! I'm so sorry!" Nadine exclaimed after her.

"Now, you've done it," Lynnette muttered under her breath, but Naomi clearly heard her.

"It was a while ago. Please don't worry." Naomi opened the door to the children's old room. "One of you can stay in here. There is a lantern and matches on the table." She walked past them to the other bedroom and opened the door but didn't look inside. "The other of you can sleep here."

A choking sensation was climbing up her throat. If she didn't get out of there fast, she could suffocate. The air was becoming thinner by the second, and she grew heady.

"Supper will be at six o'clock. We'll see you then," she managed to choke out.

She hurried from the house, letting the screen door bang shut behind her. A thin layer of sweat broke out on her upper lip. She stopped at the side door of the big house, leaning against it, trying to compose herself.

"Naomi?"

She closed her eyes.

"Naomi, are you all right?" The concern in Zach's deep voice was like another layer of heat covering her. Smothering her.

She slumped against the door, sliding down. Zach rushed to her side, grabbing her under her arms and pulling her back up. "Naomi!" he cried.

She leaned into him, and he managed to get the screen open to help her inside. He lowered her to a stool in the washroom. She dropped her head, closing her eyes.

How incredibly embarrassing. What was wrong with her? If this was going to happen when two old women asked her questions, she was going into the wrong business.

"Can you sit up by yourself?" Zach asked, bending over her as if trying to look into her eyes.

"*Jah*." She straightened her shoulders, but she was too ashamed to raise her face to him.

"All right." He left her and went into the kitchen. She heard him in the cupboard and heard the tap go on then off. He came back, holding a glass full of water. "Drink," he said. "It will make you feel better."

She took the glass and gratefully took a long drink. It did make her feel better. "I'm sorry. I don't know what got into me."

"You have new guests?"

"*Jah*. Two women."

Zach stepped back as if he wanted to get a better look at her. "Your face was white as cow's milk," he said. "It's better now."

"Thank you. For helping me, I mean."

The worry lines etched across his forehead softened. "I want to help you," he uttered, and then as if realizing what he'd just said, his cheeks colored. He took off his straw hat and ran his hand over his mouth and chin. "I'm done with my field work for the day."

A sudden sensation that the washroom was too small for the both of them came over her. She stood, feeling steadier now.

"That's *gut*."

"*Jah*." He fingered the brim of his hat. "The fencing around your pigpen needs fixing. That critter is going to escape before long."

Naomi frowned. She hadn't paid much mind to the hog lately. Ben was in charge of feeding him. "I'll get on it."

Zach reached out and touched her arm, and a deep surge of heat zapped through her. He jerked his hand back, as if he'd felt it, too. "I'll fix it. That's why I was mentioning it. So you wouldn't worry."

"But Zach, you mustn't. You lease the land. You're not responsible for fixing things around here. I can do it. You already fixed the roof."

"Naomi." His voice was firm. He pressed his hat back on his head, and stepped toward the door. "I said I'll do it. So, I'll do it."

And with that, he walked out of the house shutting the door behind him.

She stared at the closed door. Taking a step across the room, she watched him through the thin cotton curtains at the small window. His stride was long and determined. Angry-looking, almost. She shivered. Why would he be angry? There was no reason.

Was there?

Chapter Five

At ten minutes after six, when Katy was tapping her bare foot against the floor of the kitchen, there was noise at the front door.

"Finally!" Katy cried. "I'll get the food on the table."

"Thank you, daughter." Naomi went to the front door to let the two guests in. She wondered at herself when she didn't tell them that they could use the side door from then on. Was she trying to keep her distance from them?

"We're mighty hungry," said Nadine with a wide smile.

"Been itching for some Amish-cooked food," said Lynnette.

"Please come through and take a seat," Naomi directed. The women followed her to the dining area, and Naomi smiled as they both perched on the bench next to Ben.

"Hello there, young fella," Nadine said. She reached out to tussle Ben's hair, but Ben made a slight movement back and her hand dropped to her lap.

"This is my son, Ben," Naomi said quickly. "And helping with supper is my daughter, Katy."

"Nice to know you," Lynnette said, nodding. She glanced around the table, looking at the place settings.

Naomi could practically hear her counting them.

"And your husband?" the woman asked, her brows raised.

Naomi's gaze darted to both her children before answering. "He was in the accident with my father. My mother, too," she said, her voice soft. "They're all deceased."

Lynnette's eyes widened, and her cheeks turned pink. "Oh. Uh. I'm real sorry to hear that."

"Then who was the young man out in the fields earlier?" Nadine asked.

Katy blinked and turned on her heel back to the kitchen.

"That's Mr. Zach," Ben said.

Naomi put her hand on Ben's shoulder. "Zachariah King. He leases our land to farm."

"I see," Nadine said.

Katy returned with a basket of bread, but Naomi could see that her eyes were moist and her lips were pressed tightly together.

"Thank you, Katy." Naomi sat and nodded to Katy's spot. Katy sat, staring down at her plate. "Shall we say the blessing?"

During the meal, the two women kept up a constant stream of chatter. Naomi was thankful that it wasn't all questions she had to answer. She was also grateful that she didn't have to say much. Katy was completely silent, and Ben began to look sleepy enough to fall right off the bench.

Finally, after an hour of non-stop talk, the two got up and moved from the table.

"What time is breakfast?" Nadine asked.

"We can serve it at seven-thirty, unless you have a different preference," Naomi said.

"How about eight-thirty?" Lynnette asked. "Even that's a bit early."

"Now you know, Lynnette," interjected Nadine, "we need to be getting on the road."

"True. But there's time enough, I would think."

"Then, we'll say good night," Naomi said and stood. "Breakfast will be at eight-thirty."

The women looked a bit abashed, as if they didn't expect to be dismissed. Naomi supposed they'd planned to sit in the front room and talk the rest of the evening away, but Naomi knew she wouldn't be able to bear it. She hated to be ungrateful, but she wondered whether their one hundred dollars was worth the inquisition.

Justin Moore had been so much more fun as a guest.

She felt her cheeks grow warm, as she ushered the women to the front door. They said good night, and Naomi watched them go down the porch steps.

"Let me know if you need anything," she called after them, feeling almost guilty—as if she needed to offer something in return for not wanting to spend the whole evening together. But then she realized she was being silly. Surely, it wasn't necessary to entertain guests every moment of their stay.

She went to the kitchen where Katy was busy washing dishes. She walked up to her and put her arm around the young girl's shoulders. "I'm sorry, daughter. They are quite the talkers, aren't they?"

Katy nodded.

"They meant no harm."

"I know," Katy said.

"Leave these dishes. Why don't you go outside for a bit before bedtime?"

Katy pulled her hands from the water, and Naomi handed her a towel. "It'll get better, you know. Every month that passes. It'll get better."

Again, Katy nodded. Then she threw her arms around Naomi is a crushing hug. Naomi held her close for a long while. Katy didn't cry, nor did she make a sound, which was a welcome change. Used to be the girl couldn't stop weeping.

Naomi sent up a prayer of gratitude. What she'd said was true. Things *were* getting better, whether they were consciously aware of it or not. Her mind jolted back to her episode earlier when Zach had intervened. She took a slow breath and kissed the top of Katy's *kapp*. Despite what had happened that afternoon, she was getting better, too.

But she was grateful that Zach had been there. She hadn't liked him seeing her like that, but his strong hands helping her inside had been a comfort. He was a good man.

How often she thought so.

~

Naomi braced herself the next morning for the onslaught of the women at breakfast. Surprisingly, they were quiet. Both of them looked tired, and Naomi worried that they hadn't slept well or been comfortable in the *daadi haus*.

As they were checking out and paying, Naomi decided to ask them. "Did you sleep all right?"

"Neither of us ever sleep well the first night in a new place," Nadine said. She put her hand on Naomi's arm. "Now, don't you get upset about it. It had nothing to do with the accommodations. Everything was real comfortable."

"I'll put the bags in the car," Lynnette called through the door.

Nadine went on. "We want to thank you for everything. Actually, we're sorry we can't stay another night. We'll be sharing all about your place with our friends, though. So be expecting more guests." Nadine leaned close as if making an important announcement. "My book club has read quite a few Amish romances. They're going to be plum jealous of me and Lynnette. I imagine a few of them will book a stay immediately." She glanced around the top of the expansive oak desk as if searching for something. "Do you have a phone?"

Naomi shook her head. "Not yet. I will get one soon." And she realized it was true. She *would* get one soon; although, she didn't have a clue about what was involved in buying a cell phone.

"Wonderful! Why don't I give you my number and when you get a phone, you give me a call. I'll spread the word to my Book Club. My relatives, too. They'd fancy a night with the Amish."

Naomi took down Nadine's number.

"I guess that's it, then." Nadine gave her a smile. "Don't be too surprised if you see us again next year. We pass through this way every year on our way up to Chicago. We have a conference there. It's a church retreat of sorts. Why, you might be interested. It's quite—"

"Nadine!" Lynnette called from the porch. "Are you coming? We're going to be late. And you know the Chicago traffic. We'll be lucky to arrive at all!"

Nadine laughed. "Okay. I'm off. Good-bye, Naomi."

Naomi hurried with her to the door and waved them off. As the billows of dust followed them out of the drive, she couldn't help but smile. For all their nosy ways, they really were nice women. Truth be told, they weren't so different from many of her own people. After all, didn't her fellow women friends want to know everything about everyone, too?

She'd have that confirmed soon enough at the quilting frolic on Saturday.

On a whim, she decided to walk down the drive to check again on her sign. The heat of the sun wrapped itself around her like a woolen cape as she tread over the dirt and smooth stones. The warm earth felt good on her bare feet, and she swung her arms loosely at her sides, feeling almost carefree. When she got to the road, she saw the sign still standing, looking even sturdier than when she and the children had first put it up. She wondered whether it was settling into the ground.

She shaded her eyes against the sun's rays and considered the sign further. She supposed it had a bit of charm to it, despite the somewhat messy writing and amateurish appearance. Squinting her eyes, she imagined a new sign there. A beautiful carved sign, announcing Byler's Bed & Breakfast in plain box letters, all evenly done in beautiful oak wood. It would be lovely.

The whine of a car's motor coming close brought Naomi from her reverie, and she turned to go back to the house. There were still some morning chores to be done, and she thought she'd prepare a special snack for the children that morning.

A week passed with no guests. Naomi didn't mind as she had plenty to do. Attending the quilting frolic had inspired her to begin a new quilt of her own. She decided to use pieces from Isaac's and her parents' clothing. She would incorporate them into two quilts and give one to Ben and one to Katy. The idea pleased her greatly, and she couldn't wait to begin. She decided to keep her work a secret from the children and surprise them with the finished quilts. They would be right fine keepsakes.

Zachariah had been as good as his word, fixing the pigpen for them. Ben had helped, and during suppertime that evening, he had excitedly recounted how each nail was pounded. With a feeling of contentment, Naomi had watched the glimmer in his eyes and the glow on his face. Now, if she could only find a way to bring that look of pleasure to Katy's face.

"*Mamm*," Katy said, opening the screen door and coming out to join Naomi on the porch. "Can I go to see Liz? I haven't played with her for a long time."

Naomi smiled. "She can come over here to play if you'd like. You could make cookies together." Katy loved baking more than just about anything.

Katy grimaced. "Liz hates to cook."

"But does she hate to eat?" Naomi asked, with a twinkle in her eye.

Katy laughed. "She likes to eat."

"Why not go over and ask her to come? If you don't want to bake cookies, I will. Either way, you'll both get a treat."

Katy gave her a quick hug. "Thanks, *Mamm*." She skipped down the steps and was halfway to the road when she paused and turned back. "We don't have to let Ben play with us, do we?"

Naomi usually insisted that Ben be included. Katy fussed about it, but she was a fairly good sport. Naomi supposed that it was time Katy and Liz had playtime without a young brother hanging around. "No, daughter, Ben doesn't have to play with you."

Katy grinned and took off running, kicking up a few loose rocks as she sped away.

Naomi picked up a pair of Ben's trousers from the basket beside her and began to mend the hole in the knee. The patch she'd attached only the month before had already pulled loose. *Typical boy*, she mused, as she threaded her needle.

A sense of peace filled her as she sat there, rhythmically pushing and pulling the needle in and out of the fabric. There was a faint hum of insects in the air, and a slight breeze touched her face. With a start, she realized she was smiling. She was sitting there on her porch, *smiling* —for no real reason.

"Dear *Gott*, thank You," she whispered. "You truly are with us, watching over us and caring for us. Thank You."

No sooner had she spoken her prayer than she opened her eyes to see a white car coming up her drive toward the porch. Her breath caught in her throat. *A white car.*

She stood and dropped the mending to the floor.

Is it? Could it be? Impossible!

The car was close enough that she could see the driver clearly through the windshield. She saw his strong jaw, his whiskered chin, and his delighted smile. Her heart froze within her. What was he doing? Why had he come?

Her first instinct was to run inside the house, slam the door, and hide. Her second instinct was to run down the steps and greet him with her own delighted smile.

She did neither.

She stood on the edge of the porch, like a chiseled sculpture, her mind racing through possible reasons for his presence. The car engine stopped and he got out, stretching tall and again impressing her with his unusual height.

"Naomi," he said, and her name was like a melody on his lips.

She blinked, opened her mouth to speak, but nothing came forth.

"I've shocked you," he stated. He shut his car door and came around to the bottom of the steps. "I would have called, but—" He shrugged, his smile still holding. "Since there's no phone, that wasn't going to work."

He took a step up, and Naomi's pulses raced.

"Aren't you even going to greet me?" His smile shortened at the edges. "Have I made a mistake? Coming again?"

"I-I, *gut* afternoon, Justin," she stammered.

He exhaled and tilted his head. "I knew it was a risk. Me coming back so soon. But I do have a reason. I have something for you."

Her eyebrows rose. She clasped her hands to her chest, feeling completely dismayed. And excited. And afraid. And disgusted with herself for all three emotions.

Justin Moore was a *kind man*. He wasn't to be feared. He was a friend. Pure and simple. There was nothing wrong with that. Was there?

Ach! What was she to do?

He laughed, a low quiet chuckle. "Oh, Naomi, if you could see your face. The emotions playing over it would do you well in Hollywood." He laughed again. "May I sit?" He gestured with his head toward an empty rocker on the porch.

"*Jah*," she muttered, struggling to get herself under control. "Of course. How nice to see you again, Mr. Moore."

"Mr. Moore, huh?" He shrugged. "I'll take it. Better than being called an ogre or a beast or a cheeky fellow."

She frowned, unsure of what he obviously meant as a joke. "Can I get you some lemonade?"

"That would be lovely. Mighty warm today, isn't it?"

"I'll be back in a moment," she said and hurried inside. She practically ran to the kitchen in her haste to put some distance between the two of them. She grabbed the glass pitcher of lemonade from the refrigerator and snatched two glasses from the cupboard.

He had something for her? What could it possibly be? And she couldn't take gifts from a fancy man. What was he thinking? She poured the drink and taking a deep breath, she carried both glasses outside. He reached for one, and she was careful that their fingers didn't touch. He took a long drink and sighed.

"So good. Thank you, Naomi."

She sat in her rocker and raised her glass to her lips with a shaky hand. She took a small sip and then looked at him.

"I'm sorry," he said. "I can see that you're still shocked to see me."

He looked at her with his gold-flecked brown eyes—that rare color which had intrigued her weeks ago when he'd first stayed at the Bed and Breakfast. Now, he was gazing at her again, his eyes telling her how much he'd missed her. How much he cared. She could see it plain as day, and she squirmed in her chair.

"As I told you, staying here meant the world to me. I was trying to think of something I could do to help you. I have been singing your praises to anyone with half an ear." He chuckled. "And there are people who will probably stay here in the next few months because of my bragging. At least, I hope so."

"Thank you," Naomi murmured, her hands grasping her glass. She sat still, afraid to move, almost afraid to speak. Had she given the wrong impression to Justin when he was there last? Had she led him to believe...? She couldn't continue her line of thought out of fear as to where it might lead her.

Truth be told, there was something charming and magnetic about the man sitting beside her. He had a playful, curious spirit which she found refreshing and intriguing. She wouldn't soon forget the time he'd helped gather the eggs. He'd been like a child tasting candy for the first time. Just thinking about it brought a smile to her lips.

"What?" he asked, leaning slightly forward. "What's funny? You're smiling."

Her eyes widened in alarm. Was she so transparent? "Nothing," she said quickly.

He narrowed his eyes for the briefest moment and then grinned at her. "You look good, Naomi. Happy."

She nodded as discomfort tingled up her spine. She wasn't accustomed to being analyzed publically.

"I'm glad to see it. Very glad."

Before she could even begin to think about responding, she heard a clatter inside the barn. She turned, craning her neck to see if it was Ben. It wasn't. Her breath froze in her throat as Zachariah appeared at the barn door. Even at that distance, she saw the look of shock on his face upon seeing her guest. She saw his shoulders rise, and he went completely still.

Justin had followed her gaze to the barn, and he also went still. Naomi cleared her throat and searched for something to say.

Her discomfort grew as the silence stretched, but just as she despaired about what to do, Justin relaxed and said in a casual tone, "That's the man who leases your land, right? Isn't his name Zachariah something or other?"

"Zachariah King," she answered.

"So, he uses your barn, too?"

Naomi quelled the flicker of irritation his question brought forth. "He fixes things for me," she said. She had an inexplicable urge to enumerate all the different things Zach had done for her of late.

"That's nice of him," Justin said, turning toward her. "I didn't realize he did so much."

Naomi frowned. Justin's mood had changed, and she wasn't sure she wanted to go there with him. She straightened her posture and smiled. "It's a farm. Things need doing all the time."

Out of the corner of her eye, she saw Zach move. She fully expected him to retreat back to the fields, knowing he wasn't one for small talk, but she was wrong. He was heading directly toward them.

Since Zach was coming from behind, Justin seemed unaware of his approach, but Naomi saw him clearly. She saw the dark angry-looking shadows on his face. She rose to her feet, and Justin turned around to watch Zach approach along with her.

Justin stood beside Naomi. "Hello, Zachariah. How nice to see you again." He took a step down the stairs and extended his hand.

Zach closed the distance between them and shook hands, his eyes steady on the *Englischer*. "Mr. Moore." There was censure in his tone.

Zach looked up at Naomi, and she met his gaze. A thousand questions were in his eyes, but she hardly knew what to say. Justin coming hadn't been her idea.

"What brings you to Hollybrook again?" Zach asked, and there was emphasis on the word *again*.

"I have something for Mrs. Byler," Justin said, sitting back down and rubbing his hands over his thighs.

So, I am Mrs. Byler when Zach is around.

Zach's expression darkened further. "And what might that be?"

Justin turned from Zach to Naomi. "It's coming tomorrow," he said. "I do hope you like it."

"What's coming?" Zach asked, his voice louder than usual.

"It's a sign," he said. He looked at Naomi, and his eyes brightened. "I had a sign professionally made for you. I hope you like it."

"A sign?" She was stunned. How in the world did Justin know how much she wanted one?

"Yes. For your business. Often signs for B & B's are lit up, but obviously that isn't going to work for you. I ordered one to be made of wood. It's being delivered and installed tomorrow."

Naomi's lips parted but no sound came forth. She was still gaping at him, her emotions a tangled mess as she realized just how far he had overstepped.

He rushed on. "But I noticed you already have a sign. I saw it on my way in. If you don't want a new one, say the word. I didn't want to butt in."

"Butt in?" Zach asked. His face had gone completely white. Naomi had rarely seen anyone with such a pale expression. *"Butt in?"* he repeated.

"A new sign is wonderful *gut*," Naomi hastily remarked. *A new sign?* It still hadn't fully registered. "I was wanting one so badly. Thank you, Mr. Moore."

"Your feelings wouldn't be hurt, then, if the other one is removed?"

"Hardly! Katy helped me with it, but we both thought it looked quite unprofessional."

"That's wonderful." Justin gave her a warm smile. "So it is all right."

Naomi took a quick intake of breath. *Was* it all right to accept a gift from an *Englischer* like that? But how could she turn it down?

Wouldn't that be rude? Wasn't she obliged to accept a gift so freely given?

Her gaze flitted to Zach, and her chest tightened. His paleness was gone, and his face had turned red. The man looked ready to explode.

"I'd have to pay you for it, of course," she said quickly, hoping that would calm Zach down. Her mind whirled. There was no way she would be able to find money to pay for a sign.

"No." Justin frowned. "No, of course not. The whole idea was to do something nice for you. I mean, something nice for your B & B."

"You came all the way from wherever to tell her about the sign?" Zach asked. "Why didn't you write?"

Zach's words rankled Naomi. He was being downright rude. He wasn't her relative. Nor was he her bishop or preacher. He didn't have authority to be tossing out such questions.

Zach glanced at her and surely he could see the irritation on her face, but if anything, he looked more determined than ever to pursue his line of questioning. His eyes turned back to Justin.

"You're right, Zachariah," Justin said smoothly, but Naomi thought she saw his fists clench slightly. "Fact is, I had other business this way and wanted to deliver the news personally."

Zach didn't respond. He simply stood, his shoulders raised, his gaze unwavering.

"Would you like some lemonade, Zach?" Naomi asked, desperate to break the tension. "I'd be glad to get you some."

She snapped her mouth shut, stunned by the look on Zach's face. His eyes had glazed over, and if she didn't know better, he looked like he was in anguish. Something unfathomable in his eyes reached out to her, and she found herself wanting to move toward him, to step down the stairs and stand beside him. To put her hand on his arm.

He moved back a pace. "No lemonade for me. I'll be going. *Gut* day," He turned on his heel and walked away, and his shoulders visibly lowered. They sank to the point of drooping, as if weighted down with an unimaginable burden.

"Zach!" Naomi called after him.

He paused and glanced back over his shoulder.

"Thank you," she said, wondering what she was thanking him for. He raised his hand in a wave and kept walking.

"Nice to see you again," Justin called to his retreating back.

Naomi sank down to her chair, realizing she still clutched her nearly full glass of lemonade.

"He's upset," Justin observed. "I don't blame him."

A trembling started deep within Naomi's stomach. Shaking, she raised the lemonade to her lips and took a sip.

"Am I getting into the middle of something?" Justin asked, studying her.

Naomi frowned, her stomach now aching. "Of course not."

"Good. Then, do you have a vacancy?" he asked with a smile.

"*Jah*," she answered. "You can have your same room again."

"Marvelous."

"No charge, of course," she continued, swallowing past a metallic taste in her mouth. "Can you consider it a payment of sorts? For the sign, I mean."

He stared at her for a long moment and then smiled. "Yes. I would say a free night covers the sign very nicely."

Naomi knew it wasn't true. A well-done sign would cost much more than one hundred dollars, but it was all she could do right then.

"Let me grab my bag." Justin nearly leapt down the steps and went to his car. His excitement was palpable, and the acid-like taste in Naomi's mouth increased.

Chapter Six

"Why didn't you bring Liz home?" Naomi asked when Katy appeared back home alone.

"She couldn't come. Her mother had her watching her brothers." Katy shrugged. "It's okay, though. She said she could come over tomorrow."

"I'm glad to hear that."

"Why's he here? *The Englischer*, I mean," Katy asked her mother as they worked together preparing a light supper of cold cuts, home-baked bread, pickles, glazed carrots, and fresh sugar cookies.

Naomi set her bread knife down. "Katy girl, you won't believe it."

"What?"

"He's gotten us a new sign for our Bed and Breakfast. Isn't that wonderful?"

"A new sign?" Katy's forehead creased. "What do you mean?"

"He's having a new sign delivered tomorrow. You won't feel badly, will you, if we take down the one we made?"

Katy shook her head and smiled. "*Mamm*, it's still ugly."

Naomi grinned, relieved that Katy didn't seem upset, about either the sign or Justin's presence.

"But why is he giving us a sign?"

"I think he was so happy to be our first guest last month."

"But doesn't he live a long ways from here?"

"He lives in Texas."

"He sure came a long way to bring a sign." Katy shook her head.

"That he did." Naomi picked up the knife and continued slicing the bread. "But it was a nice thing to do."

Katy pursed her lips as if she was giving that a bit of thought. Then she shrugged and picked up the bowl of pickles to set on the table.

"*Mamm!*" Ben called, zooming into the kitchen from the washroom. "Where's Mr. Zach? He ain't in the fields."

Naomi turned toward her son, taking in his mussed hair and dirty trousers. "I think he went home."

Zach rarely left before suppertime. Truth be told, he often stayed well past mealtime, puttering about in the barn. She knew Zach hadn't been happy regarding Justin's presence, but it seemed odd that he would have left and not returned all afternoon.

"I wanted to show him my rock." Ben's expression drooped. "It's really a *gut* one."

"Your rock?" Katy asked, starting to laugh.

"It's not funny!" Ben cried. "Look!" He opened his fist and showed them a smooth gray stone with a copper-colored streak running through it.

"That's right pretty," Naomi said, giving Katy a look.

"*Jah*, Ben," Katy played along. "It's a nice one."

Ben's face perked up. "But I want to show Mr. Zach. He likes rocks."

"He'll be back tomorrow," Naomi said. "Now go wash up for supper. We have a guest for the night."

"Who?"

"Mr. Moore. You remember him, don't you? He stayed a few weeks back."

"*Jah*, I remember." Ben wandered back to the wash room.

"It's six o'clock. Let's get the food on the table," Naomi said.

No sooner were the dishes on the table, than Justin came in through the side door. "I'm here," he called out, walking through to the dining area.

"We're ready," Naomi said. "Won't you sit down?"

"Thank you." He smiled at the children. "Hello again, you two. It's nice to see you again."

"Hi," Ben said with a shy smile.

"Hello, Mr. Moore," Katy said.

"Shall we pray?" Naomi asked when everyone got situated. She bowed her head and felt at a total loss as to what to pray. Her feelings had been in complete turmoil since Justin had driven up to the door, and the guilt that was nagging around the edges of her heart wanted to wield its power. She gulped. Why should she feel guilty? She'd done nothing wrong.

But she *had*.

She had entertained thoughts of an *Englischer*. A fancy man. And she was feeling flattered that Justin thought enough of her to return all the way from Texas with a gift. An important gift. Something she really wanted. And she was accepting it, too.

Had she really done *nothing* wrong?

She became aware of Ben fidgeting beside her. She quickly prayed

God's blessing upon the food and cleared her throat. Everyone looked up, and Naomi started the food around the table.

~

After supper, Justin went back to the *daadi haus* and Naomi finished *redding* up the kitchen. She stood at the sink and peered through the window at the darkening night sky. The long summer days would soon be a thing of the past, and it would be time to haul out the winter capes and coats. She spotted a firefly skimming above the cut grass and smiled. "I'm going to join you outside," she whispered.

She walked past the front room where Katy and Ben were playing a game of checkers, slipped outside to the porch, and settled into one of the rockers. She took a long slow breath and gazed out across the lawn. Her *dat* and husband had chosen well. The farm was beautiful, and the land was rich and fertile. The trees gracing the front yard had stood for decades, and their fluttering leaves sheltered birds and insects and provided shade when the summer temperatures rose into the nineties.

She let out her breath. The night noises were quiet and restful. She heard the faint sound of a horse's clip clop on the road, and she wondered which of her neighbors was taking a night drive and why. For a moment, she forgot about her guest; she forgot about Zach's earlier dismay; she forgot about the bills piling up on her husband's oak desk.

She closed her eyes and just let herself be.

"Naomi?"

She jerked upright. Justin stood at the bottom of the stairs, smiling up at her.

"*Ach*, Justin. I didn't hear you."

He climbed the steps and sat beside her. "I'm sorry. I didn't mean to startle you."

"*Nee*. It's all right." But it wasn't. She wanted to forget he was there. She wanted to pretend that all was well again between her and Zach.

She wanted to pretend that she could never have feelings for this man of the world who was sitting much too close.

"I missed you," he said, his voice low but tense.

She sucked in a quick breath and wished with all her heart that he hadn't spoken.

"Will you look at me?" he asked, whispering now.

She turned toward him and flinched at the passion reflected in his eyes. Every muscle in her body stiffened, and her throat went dry.

"I know I shouldn't say such things. Well, at least I think I shouldn't. I've been studying the Amish on the Internet, trying to find out all I can about your way of life."

He had? *To what end?*

"I find your culture and your belief system fascinating."

She stared at him, unblinking. She needed to stop this line of conversation and right quick. Nothing good could come of it.

"The weather is cooling down these days, don't you think?"

He winced, and then he closed his mouth. His eyes searched hers, and she forced herself not to look away. She saw the torment revealed in the depths of his gaze. She saw the conflict there. His unrest appeared as deep as hers. A silence fell between them as they continued to stare at one another. Naomi's heart contracted, and a sadness moved through her. Not the crushing sadness she'd carried since her husband's accident. No, this was different.

It was a reluctant sadness, a knowing sadness, a bittersweet sadness that filled her at once with both regret and gratitude. This man... This lovely man beside her was giving her more than a new sign. He was giving her hope. Hope that she could love someone again.

Not in the same that she had loved Isaac. No. Isaac had been her first love. She had gone from her parent's loving care to his. She would never love someone the same way she'd loved Isaac.

When she loved again, it would be a different love. Perhaps a more tender love. And for certain, a more grateful love. But a solid love, too, and passionate. That would be the same.

Justin reached out and took her hand in his. She allowed it, knowing that somehow they were communicating beyond words. Beyond convention. Beyond rules.

The sadness she felt—she saw it in his eyes, too. She saw his love there, also, and she was touched and deeply grateful. As he continued to look at her, she saw the moment when his final resignation set in. His expression wilted, and he *knew*. He knew that it would never work between the two of them. He knew it would never be possible.

"Oh, Naomi. You don't want the sign, do you?" His voice was low and thick, and his eyes filled with tears.

She didn't answer right away, but she gently peeled his fingers away from her hand. She took her palm from his and clasped her hands in her lap. He looked down at his own empty hand for a long minute, and then he looked back up to her.

"It was a crazy thought," he said. "A longshot. The longest shot ever. But I had to try. You understand that, don't you?"

She had trouble swallowing around the growing lump of tears in her throat. She nodded her head.

"It's like a force driving me," he continued. His eyes held her. "Forgive me for saying this, but I love you, Naomi Byler."

Her fingers tightened around each other in a claw grip.

He shook his head. "You don't have to say anything. In fact, I don't want you to say anything. But I had to tell you. I *had* to." He spoke the last three words slowly, over-enunciating each one. "If your world were different ... if my world were different ... I think we would have stood a real chance."

He shook his head and rubbed his hand over his mouth. Then he lowered his hand again to his side, he went on. "I know you care for me. It's in your eyes." He blinked and a tear rolled down his cheek. "Now, sitting here with you again, in your world, I see that it's not enough. My love isn't enough. It will never be enough. Our worlds will never be bridged. Love alone can't do that."

Naomi's lips quivered. He reached over and touched her hand.

"No, Naomi, don't worry. I'm not hurt. Sad, yes. *Unbearably sad.* But I see it clearly tonight. I know, now that I look at you, that it won't work. How I wish it would. You'll never know how much I wish it would. But thank you." His voice choked up, and he paused before continuing. "Thank you for the best five days of my life." He shook his head. "Six, now, I guess."

Naomi's eyes welled with tears, and she could hardly see through them to gaze at him. She was filled with such emotion, such tenderness for him, that she couldn't speak.

"I will leave first thing in the morning. Without breakfast. I'll be gone before you even get up. And I'll cancel the sign installation. I don't want you to worry about anything." He stood and gazed down at her, and she thought her heart would break with the poignancy of it all.

He stepped away then, but she scrambled up and pulled on his hand. Standing on her tiptoes, she broke across all rules of behavior and kissed him gently on the cheek. She felt his stubby whiskers as she lingered there for one sweet moment.

He sucked in his breath and stood frozen.

She backed away. "Thank you," she whispered. "Thank you, Justin Moore."

He touched his forehead in a salute and walked slowly and quietly around the house in the growing darkness. When he disappeared from sight, Naomi sank back into her rocker and closed her eyes. She murmured a prayer, asking for forgiveness. She had started down a path of no return, and she was repentant for that. And then, she thanked God. She thanked him for His love and His mercy and His grace. She thanked Him that she was alive.

She covered her mouth in shock and began rocking, starting slowly and gaining in speed, until the rocker was rapidly creaking back and forth. *I am grateful to be alive.* She hadn't been grateful for life in months. Not since the accident. Something inside her was cracking open, and she marveled at the budding joy that was being released. She felt like running through the fields with her arms stretched wide. She felt like wiggling into the tire swing and flying up to the sky. Tears rolled down her cheeks, and she smiled up at the stars.

She glanced around to the corner of the house where Justin had vanished. "Thank you," she whispered. "Thank you. Thank you. Thank you."

~

Justin was as good as his word. By the time Naomi arose, his car was gone. She stared down at the empty spot where his car had been parked, and she wondered how far down the road he had gone. She wished him Godspeed, and then she quickly dressed to get about her chores.

In the kitchen, she pulled the bowl of eggs from the refrigerator. It would just be the three of them that morning. She glanced up at the clock. It was plenty early, and she felt an urge to gather up the dirty sheets and towels from the *daadi haus.*

Justin Moore was gone, never to return. She wanted to wash everything up. She padded outside through the side door and entered the *daadi haus.* It was still fairly dark, but she knew every inch of the house. In the bedroom, she saw that Justin had already stripped the bed and folded the quilt at the end of the mattress. She gathered up the sheets, when something caught her eye.

Bending over, she saw a one hundred dollar bill on top of a folded piece of paper. She sank onto the bed, and holding the note close to the window, she read.

Since you won't be taking the sign, I wanted to pay you for my night here. Naomi, thank you for everything. Everything. I will remember you till my dying day. I hope you'll be happy. I know you will be. I also know that you won't be alone for long. He loves you, you know.

My deepest regards,

Justin

Naomi pressed his note to her chest and felt tears sting the back of her eyes. *I will remember you, too*, she thought. *Forever.*

She stood and tucked the note and the money into her apron. *He loves you, you know.* She gazed out the window and watched the pink sky spread across the horizon as the sun climbed into a new day.

Zach.

Did he love her? She wasn't sure. Possibly. She scooped up the sheets and went into the bathroom and snatched Justin's wet towel from the rung.

Zach.

A slow smile crept over her face. He'd be arriving soon to work in the fields, and she realized that she was excited to see him. His presence on the farm was a comfort. She liked him there. Liked the way he interacted with Ben. Liked his steady ways.

He loves you, you know.

She hugged the laundry to her chest and slipped out of the *daadi haus.* The contented smile remained on Naomi's face all the way into the big house and all the way upstairs to wake the children.

The End

NAOMI'S CHOICE

Chapter One

A man's heart deviseth his way: but the Lord directeth his steps.
Proverbs 16:9 (King James Version)

Naomi stood on the porch and stared at the empty parking spot under the elm tree. Early that morning, Justin Moore's white sedan had been parked there. But true to his word, he was long gone. Naomi closed her eyes and exhaled with a heavy, relieved sigh.

It was over. He would never return. She pressed her hands over her heart and forgave herself for her wild imaginings over the last few weeks. She'd known from the first moment there was no hope of a relationship with an *Englischer*, but he'd been charming. Truth be told, he'd been *more* than charming.

But it wasn't right. Nor was it possible, and surprisingly, she felt that her heart was awakening to someone else. Her eyes misted over, and she prayed that it wasn't too soon to feel such stirrings. Isaac had only been gone a year, and she still missed him, and so did her two children.

She straightened her back. But Isaac *was* gone, and she *was* alone. She hated to admit how lonely she often felt—how long the nights stretched in her wide empty bed. How, even in the late summer, her feet grew cold, and Isaac's legs weren't there to warm them up.

A distinct clip clop sounded, and she turned to see Mary coming up the drive. Naomi stepped down the stairs and shaded her eyes as her friend approached.

"Mary!" she said with pleasure. "How nice to see you."

Mary's face was a study of concern. "Naomi Byler, what in the world did you do to Zach?"

Naomi blanched. "To Zach? What do you mean?"

Mary pulled up on the reins, and her pony jerked to a stop. She scrambled out of the cart and took Naomi's arm, pulling her up the steps and onto the porch. She collapsed into a rocking chair and indicated that Naomi should do the same.

"What's going on?" Naomi asked, becoming concerned. She hadn't done a thing to Zachariah King. Although now that she thought about it, after he'd left her fields early the day before, he hadn't returned.

"I know Zach is only leasing your fields. But as I've hinted many times, I think he's sweet on you..."

Naomi flushed. Where Zach King was concerned, her thoughts usually ended up in a confused mess. Zach had been strangely communicative lately, not to mention, he had been spending a lot of time with her five-year-old son. Of course, Ben loved it. The poor boy had been starving for male attention ever since his father had passed.

"I saw Zach mid-afternoon," Mary went on. "By the look on his face, his world had turned upside down *and* inside out."

Naomi's flush deepened. She knew he'd been upset about Justin Moore visiting her again and staying in her Bed and Breakfast.

"The man often won't speak a word, as you well know." Mary smoothed her apron over her lap. "But yesterday, he talked. I nearly swooned dead away. Said he was making a sign for you."

Naomi's eyes went wide. "A sign?" she uttered.

"*Jah*. For your Bed and Breakfast."

"*Nee. Nee.*" She shook her head. Zach was making her *a sign?*

"What happened?"

Naomi collapsed against the back of the rocker. "*Ach*, Mary. What a right fine muddle this is."

Mary frowned. "How about you tell me what's happened."

"Justin Moore stayed sat my Bed and Breakfast last night."

"Justin... Wait, ain't he that *Englischer* fellow? Wasn't he your first guest?"

"*Jah.*"

"What was he doing back here?"

Naomi groaned. "He came to bring me a gift."

Mary's eyebrows shot up to the top of her forehead. "A gift?"

"I didn't take it." Naomi paused. At first, she'd agreed to take it. In fact, she'd been glad for it. Excited. But in the end, she realized it wasn't right. Accepting that gift would have opened a door she didn't dare walk through. She sighed deeply, not wanting Mary to know all those details. "Justin ordered a sign made for my Bed and Breakfast. It was to be delivered today."

Mary began rocking, pushing her plain black shoes against the porch boards. "Mercy sakes. Mercy sakes."

"What exactly did Zach say to you?"

"Not much. Just what I said, that he was making you a sign."

Naomi blew out her breath.

"He's sweet on you." Mary stopped rocking and leaned forward. "He's a *gut* man, Naomi. A right *gut* man."

"I know. I know that, Mary."

"What are you going to do?"

Naomi squeezed her hands together on her lap. "I have no idea."

Mary stood and brushed imaginary dust off her apron. "Well, I wanted you to know what he said. Now, I've delivered my message, and I need to be getting back to my own chores."

Naomi jumped up. "Thank you for telling me."

Mary took a step down and then turned back to Naomi. "This *Englischer*. He coming back again?"

Naomi saw the worry on her face. "*Nee*. He's not coming back anymore."

Mary nodded. "*Gut*." And with that she clambered back into her cart, clucked her tongue, and rode away.

Naomi sank back in her rocker. So Zach had been making her a sign. No wonder he'd reacted so strongly when Justin announced *his* gift of a sign. She grimaced. But why hadn't Zach said anything about it to her? Was she supposed to read his mind? She gripped the arms of the rocker and shook her head. The man was beyond frustrating. One minute, he would act tender with her, and the next, he was like a cold brick walking away in silence.

She remembered her recent conversation with Mary when her friend had told her about Zach's first love, Marcy. That girl had stomped on his heart but good. While Naomi listened to the story, she'd been angry at Marcy, wondering how anyone could be so cruel.

Now, she wondered whether Zach considered *her* cruel. But still, how was she supposed to know about his sign if he didn't tell her. Making a quick decision, Naomi rose and walked down the steps and out to the barn. On the way, she scanned the fields, looking for Zach. It didn't take long to spot him. He was out in the far right field, bending over the fence. It was hard to make out what he was doing from that distance, but she supposed the fence needed mending again. The posts were old and half-rotten, and Zach was always fussing with them. Naomi wondered why he bothered. It wasn't as if a herd of wild cattle was going to trample through and crush his crops. But the previous owners had put the fences up, and Zach felt obliged to maintain them.

Naomi hesitated for a moment, watching him. He cut a fine figure out there. Tall and sturdy. She closed her eyes and visualized his stark blue eyes gazing at her. He had a way of looking into her as if he saw her very heart. It was unnerving to say the least. But she found herself seeking him out, wanting him to see her, hoping he would come by.

She shivered. All this was too much. She'd thought when she'd married Isaac that she was finished with all this courtship business. *Courtship business?* Was *that* what she was thinking? Was she falling for Zach? Did she think he was fixing to *court her*? She turned toward the barn and went inside. Whether she was falling for him or not, she wasn't going to be the cause of his pain. She wasn't going to add to the hurt Marcy had inflicted on him all those years ago.

She grabbed a shovel and carried it down the drive to the road. The sorry-looking Bed and Breakfast sign she and her eleven-year-old daughter Katy had made was still staunchly in place. Naomi began digging up the rocky dirt around its base. They'd planted it deep to ensure it wouldn't fall over, something she regretted right then as she worked through the stony ground.

The late summer sun could still pack quite a sizzle, and it wasn't long before she'd worked up a sweat. She was nearing the base of the sign now, and it was leaning precariously to the side. One more shovelful ought to do it. She was glad she wasn't barefoot like usual. Using a shovel without shoes wasn't a pleasant experience.

She shoveled the last clump of dirt from the hole, and the sign gently lay over onto the ground. The poor thing looked like a felled tree. She gave it a grateful smile.

"You may be ugly, but you did manage to bring in a few customers," she said. She bent down and pulled it from the hole, wondering whether she should leave it lying there or take it back to the barn along with the shovel.

"What are you doing?"

Naomi spun around and faced Zachariah. He stood with his legs apart and a look of confusion on his face.

"I thought you were out in the field," she exclaimed.

"I needed some wire for the fence." He took a step closer, and she was deeply aware of his scent of work and fields and hot sun.

"Oh." She swallowed.

"Won't those sign people take care of this? Surely, that fancy place the *Englischer* hired doesn't expect you to pull out the old sign yourself." The disdain in his voice sounded unnatural coming from his lips.

She straightened her shoulders. "You don't think so?" His sarcasm sparked something in her, and she found herself rankling under his gaze. "How would you know?"

His jaw twitched, and his eyes darkened. "I *don't* know."

"I thought I'd make things easier for them," she snapped, wondering what in the world she was doing. Why didn't she simply tell him that she'd refused the sign? That it wasn't going to be delivered at all.

"Where's your guest?" Zach asked, his voice stiff.

"Not here." Again, why didn't she simply tell him that Justin Moore had left? *For good.*

Zach bent over and picked up the old sign. Without a word, he hoisted it onto his shoulder and headed back to the barn. Naomi scrambled to catch up, annoyed with both herself and him. Why couldn't they have a civil conversation? Why must everything concerning Zachariah King be so *hard*?

He lumbered into the barn and tossed the sign against the wall. He turned and took the shovel from her hand and set it beside the rake and hoe. She regarded him and wondered at his obvious anger. Was it all about the sign? And just when did he plan to tell her about the one *he* was making?"

"For your information, Justin left," she blurted.

Zach's gaze settled on her face. She saw his lips tighten, and she knew he was trying to read her.

"Did you hear me?" she asked.

"I heard you." He continued to assess her.

Her pulse was racing, and her throat went dry. *Now.* Now was the perfect time for him to say something, *anything* that might give her an idea of his intentions, but he didn't speak. Naomi couldn't take her eyes from his. It was as if he'd pulled her into some kind of vortex, and she was struggling to keep her head above water.

Finally, he spoke. "He coming back?"

She shook her head.

"When's his sign coming?"

"It's not."

He stiffened, and his brow furrowed. "What?"

"It's not coming," she repeated.

"So, why'd you dig up that one?" he asked, motioning toward the old sign with a nod of his head.

Frustration surged through her. She wanted to shake him—shake him until he lost that dark curtain he wore over his face. Shake him until he admitted he was making a sign for her.

"*You tell me*," she said, stretching up even taller.

He gaped at her, and she saw a dawning come over his face. "Mary," he muttered. He let out his breath in a heavy sigh.

"*Jah*, Mary. And why not you? Why didn't *you* tell me? Was it to be a surprise?"

He shook his head, staring at her. "Not a surprise."

"So why not tell me?"

He blew out his breath. "It isn't done."

She closed her mouth, taken back. That made perfect sense. "So, you were going to tell me when it was done?"

"*Nee.*" He tapped his hat a bit lower on his forehead. "I was just going to set it up for you."

"But why didn't you say something about it yesterday when Justin told me about his sign?"

He frowned. "Really? You wanted me to say something then?"

She was glaring at him now. Did he care for her or not? And if he did, why didn't he make any effort to make himself clear? Why did he just rumble about the farm, watching her when he thought she wasn't looking?

Disgusted with the entire subject, she swirled on her heel and marched out of the barn back to the house. She had been married. She wasn't used to this kind of bantering and maneuvering. She wasn't a teenager anymore—she was a grown mother of two. She stomped up the steps of the porch and flung open the screen door. Striding inside, she went straight to the kitchen and dug out the ingredients for a massive batch of cookies.

She had a sudden hankering for something sweet.

Chapter Two

"*Mamm!*" Ben called as he raced into the front room. "How come the sign's in the barn?"

Naomi looked up from her ledger. "I took it down."

"But how come?"

"Benjamin, look at the floor. You've done tracked in a barrelful of dirt!"

Ben looked down at his thick-soled shoes. Clumps of dirt clung to their sides, some of which had fallen to the floor. He gazed behind himself at the trail he'd left. "Sorry."

"Get the broom."

"But why's the sign down."

"Because Mr. King is making us a new one." She set down her pencil, happy to take a break from her figuring.

Ben's face lit up. "He is? *Gut*! He can do anything."

A weariness settled over Naomi. "*Jah*, I suppose he can."

"He gonna stay for supper again?"

"*Nee*," she answered before he could go further with the idea. The very last thing she wanted was another confrontation with Zachariah King.

"Why not?"

"Ben, don't question your elders. Now, go get that broom."

"Okay." He hung his head slightly and turned to go. Then he swirled back to face her. "But *Mamm*, Mr. Zach loves your cooking. He said so."

Naomi sighed. "Ben? The broom?"

"I'm going," he mumbled, heading off to the washroom.

Naomi looked at her page of figures. She needed to buy a calculator; all this adding and subtracting was giving her a headache. Lots of Amish folk used calculators that ran on batteries. She'd even heard tell of calculators that used the sun to work. She never could figure why her *dat* opposed it so. Maybe because ciphering came easy to him, but it surely didn't come easily to her. She picked up her pencil and squared her shoulders to tackle it again.

She glanced out the front window and saw a billow of dust accompany a light green car coming up the drive. She set the pencil back down and went out to greet whomever it was. More guests, perhaps?

The car came to a stop, and a young man got out.

"Howdy, ma'am," he said with a wide smile. "We're looking for Byler's Bed and Breakfast. We stopped a ways back and someone directed us here."

"You've come to the right place," she said, excitement stirring in her chest. She wondered how this young couple even knew of her Bed and Breakfast, especially since she'd taken down the sign. But that didn't matter. They were there. "How can I help you?"

"We're wanting to stay a couple of nights." His voice carried a heavy drawl, reminding her of Justin's way of speaking. "The missus and me."

The passenger window came down and a lovely young woman with glistening red hair poked her head through the opening. "I'm Gladys," she said with the same drawl, only softer. "Please no jokes about my name. My mother seemed to think it amusing to slap an ancient-style name on me."

Naomi's brows rose, and she shook her head. "Gladys is a fine name." How odd for someone to jump right into such talk after introducing themselves. Naomi would have thought such comments would be reserved for dear friends.

"So, you know Justin Moore?" the man asked, coming around his car.

At the mention of Justin's name, Naomi's heart skipped a beat. Justin had told her that he would send guests her way, but she never truly expected it. She thought he was being kind, trying to encourage her. And after their parting of ways, she assumed he would put her out of his mind forever.

"*Jah*," she murmured. "I know Justin Moore."

"He can't stop raving about your place," Gladys said. Her eyes roamed the area. "It is lovely here. He certainly got that right."

She opened her door and stepped out. Her long tanned legs were thin, and she had on a pair of orange slip-on shoes. She wore a snug short dress with geometric shapes printed all over it. She tossed her fiery hair back over her shoulders and gave a contented sigh.

"I'm simply going to love it here," she said. "Please tell us you have a vacancy."

Naomi nodded. "*Jah*, we have a vacancy. Two nights did you say?"

The man offered her his hand, and she shook it. Would she ever get used to touching strangers?

"I'm Scott," he said. "Is it true that you have no electricity?"

"*Jah*, that's true. Do you still want to stay?"

Gladys laughed, a joyous tinkling sound. "It will do us good to unplug," she said, nudging Scott. "Won't it, honey?"

"If you say so." He smiled at Naomi. "No, she's right. We've been working way too hard. Both of us. This will do us good."

"If you'd like to get your bags, I'll show you to your room."

"Will we stay in the same little house where Justin stayed? He said it was the coziest place he's ever slept in."

Naomi's heart warmed. "*Jah*. The same place."

When they entered the *daadi haus*, Gladys threw out her arms and practically squealed. "Yes! It truly is cozy. Where do we sleep?"

Taking a breath, Naomi took them to the bedroom she used to share with Isaac. She braced herself for the onslaught of emotions as she offered them her former bed, but when she opened the bedroom door, she felt nothing. She blinked rapidly, and her brow creased. She paused, her hand on the doorknob, waiting. She hadn't opened this door without a rush of grief and longing since the accident had happened that took her husband's life. But right then, she felt as if she were opening any other bedroom door. She was so taken back, she could hardly focus on the matter at hand.

Gladys moved past her. "This is a charming room," she said. She went to the lantern sitting on a bedside table. "Here's our light, honey!"

Scott joined her. "The old-fashioned kind," he said with a chuckle. "I'm looking forward to this."

Gladys faced Naomi. "Do you have hot water for a shower? I should have asked in the beginning."

"We do," Naomi said, blinking hard and bringing herself back into the moment.

Gladys's shoulders relaxed. "I hate to be prudish, but I do like a hot shower."

Scott rubbed his hands together. "Justin told us it was one hundred fifty a night because you add in meals."

One hundred fifty? Naomi blanched. Justin knew full well it was only one hundred dollars a night.

"*Nee.* It's only—"

Scott was already peeling three one hundred dollar bills from his wallet. He handed them to her. "This will cover two nights. I can get a receipt from you at dinner."

Naomi stepped back, but he pressed the money into her palm.

"But this is too much," she said.

"Hardly," Scott replied. "Not if meals are included. We want to hole up here for the next couple days. Not having to go out for meals is a real plus."

Naomi stood dumbfounded. Even when he wasn't around, Justin was making his mark.

"What time is dinner?" Gladys asked. "We don't want to be late."

"Six o'clock. But really, this is too much money."

"Nonsense. We'll see you at six," Scott said, placing their compact suitcase on the end of the bed.

Naomi was being dismissed from her own *daadi haus*, which was a switch, but she found she didn't mind. *Three hundred dollars.* Was this Justin's way of telling her she was charging too little? No, she didn't think so. This was Justin's way of thanking her once again. She held the money to her chest as she went back to the big house, grateful that Justin Moore was still her friend even though she'd never see him again.

"Thank you, *Gott*," she whispered as she went in to prepare supper. She took the green beans out of the refrigerator and set about snapping them. As she worked, her mind rested on Justin. She realized that thinking of him wasn't painful anymore. There was no yearning, no wishing things could be different. Instead, she felt a contentment at knowing him, a gentle gratitude for their time together.

And that was all.

Humming now, she set on a pot of water. Beans took quite a bit of boiling to become tender and tasty.

~

Katy wandered into the kitchen an hour before supper was to be served. "On my way back from Liz's house, I stopped by the mailbox. You got a letter from Uncle Marvin."

Naomi sighed. She already knew what was in the letter. Marvin would be pressuring her once again to move back to Pennsylvania. That was his standard fare.

"Set it on the counter. I'll get to it later." She handed Naomi the bread knife. "Would you cut the loaf and put some slices on a plate?"

"Sure, *Mamm*. Do we have guests? There's a car out front. And what happened to our sign on the road?"

"Mr. Zach is making us a new sign. And yes, we do have guests. For two nights. A nice young couple."

Katy grinned. "We're doing *gut*, aren't we? We're getting money?"

Naomi regarded her. "I don't want you worrying about money, daughter. Things are fine."

Katy's face flushed. "I'm not little anymore."

Naomi stepped closer. "I know that."

"I heard you talking to Mrs. Mary once. You told her we needed the money. You've said the same thing to Ben and me, too."

Naomi blew out her breath. "Katy, you leave those concerns to me. The Good Lord has taken care of us so far, hasn't He?"

Katy pressed her lips together and nodded.

"And He'll continue to take care of us." She squeezed Katy's shoulders. "Now, that bread isn't going to slice itself."

Katy grinned and starting cutting the bread.

Supper was ready a few minutes before six. Ben had skipped in and washed up and was already waiting on the long bench, his legs swinging beneath the heavy table. Naomi and Katy set out the creamed potatoes, green beans, bread, fried chicken, and sliced carrots.

"This is more like dinner than supper," Katy said.

"Smells good," Ben exclaimed with an appreciative sniff.

"They're paying well," Naomi said, "so I want to make sure they eat well."

"Hello!" Scott called through the door. "Are you ready for us?"

Naomi went to let them in. "*Gut* afternoon. Come straight in."

Scott and Gladys entered the dining area and both of them let out an exclamation of pleasure. "Oh, this looks wonderful," Gladys said.

"Please be seated," Naomi said. "These are my two children, Ben and Katy." She turned to her children. "Ben and Katy, this is Mr. Scott and Mrs. Gladys."

Ben and Katy nodded and smiled.

Scott and Gladys got situated, and Naomi directed them all in a silent prayer of thanks. When she cleared her throat, everyone looked up. Naomi was always surprised when new guests fell so easily into their Amish manner of saying grace. She knew most *Englischers* said grace out loud, something she'd never done before.

"Start the creamed potatoes around, would you Ben?" she asked.

The meal went well. As it turned out, Scott and Gladys were pleasant conversationalists. Ben had quite a time sharing his knowledge of frogs, once Scott caught on about how important frogs were to the lad.

When everyone was finished eating, her guests went straight back to the *daadi haus,* and she sent Katy and Ben outside for a bit of playtime before bed. She yearned for the quiet of her kitchen to *red* everything up for the morning and to read Marvin's letter. After the last dish was put away, and the breakfast meal was planned, she took the letter from the counter and sat down in the kitchen rocker to read it.

Dear Naomi,

I hope this finds you well. I'm going to come right to the point. As you know, I've never approved of you staying in Indiana after the accident. You belong back here with your family. I don't think it's right that you are depriving your two children of their kin.

Naomi dropped the letter in her lap and looked out the kitchen window. She shouldn't get so upset at her brother's words; she'd read them often enough. How she wished he would stop pressuring her. Didn't he know that she was trying to do the right thing for her children? Didn't he know that she didn't want to upset them with another huge change in their lives?

She grabbed up the letter again, and her teeth clenched.

I've decided to come out to fetch you myself, Naomi. By the time you get this letter, I'll be on my way. I felt that I should at least give you a warning that I'm coming.

A warning! Even *he* phrased it as a warning. She shook her head. Nothing good was going to come from this; she could feel it in her bones.

The rest of the family is in agreement. So, I shall see you soon.

Your brother,

Marvin

Naomi stuffed the letter back in the envelope and stood up. She looked about her, wondering what she could do. Marvin coming there? And he didn't know about the Bed and Breakfast. She was sure he wouldn't like it one bit. He wouldn't approve of her running any type of business.

She tossed the envelope back on the counter and rushed out the side door. Once outside, she stood, looking restlessly about her. Perhaps a short walk to the fields would help ease her frustration. She certainly couldn't let the children see her upset.

She strode across the yard and around back of the barn. She went to the edge of the field and stopped, gazing out upon all of Zachariah's hard work. The corn had grown taller even in those last few days. Soon, it would be harvest time. And then the fields would be put to bed, and there would be no need for Zachariah to come around every day.

"Naomi?"

She whirled to face Zach. "*Ach*, I didn't hear you." She licked her lips and smoothed down her apron.

"What's wrong?"

She shook her head. "Wrong? Nothing's wrong."

He put down the hoe he was carrying and stepped closer. "What's wrong?" he repeated.

She turned back toward the field and watched the corn sway ever so slightly in the breeze. Dusk was creeping over the land, and she heard

Ben and Katy hollering and laughing back by the tire swing. Zach stood close and gazed out over the fields with her.

"The fields are beautiful," she murmured. "Nearly ready for harvest."

"It'll be a while yet," Zach said, his quiet tone matching hers. "I love this time in the season. Things are ripening and growing fat with the summer sun."

She nodded, glancing at him from the corner of her eye. Such poetic words, and she had never, even for a second, considered Zach a poetic man.

"Naomi?" he said, turning to her. "What's wrong?"

Her shoulders slumped. "I've heard from my brother."

"*Jah?*"

"He's coming." She closed her eyes and inhaled slowly.

"But that's right nice for you, isn't it? And for Ben and Katy?"

"*Nee.*"

His brow furrowed. "Why not?"

"He wants us to move back to Pennsylvania. He's been after me about it since the accident."

Zach inhaled sharply, and Naomi felt him go stiff beside her. "To Pennsylvania?"

She nodded. Standing there, on the land that her father and husband had so desired, had worked so hard to acquire, made Naomi realize how much she wanted to stay. How could she desert their dream? How could she leave Isaac, whose body lay in the cemetery not so far down the road? And how could she leave her mother and father, who lay in that same cemetery? No, her life was there, in Hollybrook.

Tears blurred her vision, and she made no move to stop them from falling.

"Do you want to go back?" Zach asked.

"This is my home."

Zach turned and squarely faced her. She looked into his eyes and even in the growing dusk, she could see how his gaze burned into hers. "You didn't answer," he said. "Do you want to go?"

She shook her head. "*Nee*. I want to stay."

He raised his hand and touched her arm, and it was as if her skin came alive beneath his fingers. Electricity raced up her spine, and she barely stopped herself from jerking back with surprise. She looked down at his hand, his muscled, rough hand that worked from sun-up to sun-down.

The tension between them thickened, and she swallowed and wondered what he could be thinking. And then he took his hand from her and lowered it to his side.

"When's he coming?"

She shook her head and looked up at him. "I don't know. It could be any day."

He nodded. "I'll be here, out in the fields. If you need me..."

She blinked rapidly and pinched her lips together. A yearning pressed into her chest, and she fought the urge to walk into his arms. Stunned and more than a little disturbed by her emotions, she stepped back.

"*Jah*. Out in the fields," she murmured.

His gaze lingered on her for another long moment, and then he turned and left. He walked slowly away, his movements stiff and awkward, as if he didn't want to go.

Chapter Three

"Uncle Marvin!" Ben hollered and threw open the front door. He rushed down the steps and nearly leapt into Marvin's arms.

Marvin stood outside the white van and grinned. He picked Ben up and gave him a huge bear hug. "Little man, you're growing up right fine!"

Naomi stood at the top of the porch and watched them. Marvin hadn't changed in the year or so that she hadn't seen him. He was still lanky and the corners of his brown eyes crinkled into a fistful of wrinkles. His dark beard, streaked with a bit of gray, was perhaps longer. He never saw the point of trimming it and just let it flow with its jagged length.

Marvin put Ben down and tousled his hair. Then he looked up at Naomi and gave her a smile. Naomi thought she sensed hesitation there, before he strode up the steps to greet her.

"Sister, it's good to see you." He put his arm around her shoulders and gave her a quick squeeze. "Where's Katy?"

Naomi craned her neck to gaze around toward the side of the house.

"She was in the *daadi haus* doing some cleaning." She looked at Ben. "Ben, go fetch your sister."

Ben ran off, and Naomi led Marvin inside. "Can I get you something? Are you hungry?"

He set down his suitcase and regarded her. "*Nee*. The driver stopped a couple hours back, and we ate at a restaurant. I'm fine."

Naomi ran her hands over her dress and inhaled deeply. "Why not come into the front room then and have a seat."

Marvin stretched a bit, his long arms reaching toward the ceiling. "I been sitting for what seems like a week in that van. Could do with a bit of a walk. I'd like to see the place."

"Of course," Naomi said. Her heart was fluttering as she fought down her nervousness. She was being silly; it was only her brother, after all. "Shall we go back outside?"

"Uncle Marvin!" Katy said. "You're here!"

Marvin opened his arms to her, and she rushed forward to give him a hug. "You've grown." He put his hands on her shoulders and looked her up and down. "One day soon you'll be married with your own *kinner*."

Katy blushed. "I'm not yet twelve, you know."

Marvin laughed. "Still. You're getting mighty big."

"We're going to show Marvin the farm," Naomi said. She stepped outside and started toward the barn, and the three of them followed her.

"So, you were cleaning the *daadi haus*?" Marvin asked.

"*Jah*, our last guests left this morning," Katy said.

Naomi stiffened. She hadn't yet had time to tell Marvin about the Bed and Breakfast. Her jaw tightened. Truth be told, she could have written Marvin and the family and shared that news many times, but she'd always chosen to conveniently forget about it. She regretted that decision now.

"Guests?"

They were in the barn now, and Naomi nearly choked when she saw the old Byler's Bed and Breakfast sign tossed to the side of the barn. Marvin must have noticed it at the exact same moment.

"What's this?" he asked, staring back at Naomi.

"We got a Bed and Breakfast," Ben chimed in. "That's how we met Mr. Justin. He was our first guest. He's nice. And the last two people were nice, too. 'Cept we hardly saw 'em. Only when it was time to eat."

Marvin bent down and picked up the crude sign. He turned to Naomi and stared holes through her.

"Children," Naomi said, averting her gaze. "Why don't you take Marvin's suitcase up to the spare room? Katy, you can start on supper."

"But, *Mamm*, he just got here," complained Bed. "I ain't even showed him where Mr. Zach and I find frogs."

"There'll be plenty of time for that," Naomi said. "Now, off with you."

Katy pulled on Ben's arm and the two of them hurried off, leaving an expanse of awkward silence behind them. Naomi braced herself for what was to come.

"What's this about, Naomi?"

"I've started a business," she said, attempting to put on a professional-sounding tone.

"I gathered that," he said. His brown eyes grew dark, and he narrowed them to a near squint. "Why?"

"Because I need the money." Naomi raised her chin. "And before you get all upset, you should know the bishop has approved of it. I've spoken with him, and he is in favor."

The words raced from her mouth as she tried to cut off his objections before they began, but it didn't work.

"This farm needs to be sold. You need to come home."

She stiffened. "*Nee*. This is where I live now. This is where *Mamm* and *Dat* are buried! My husband is buried here. I can't leave."

Marvin stepped toward her. "Ruth and I have spoken about it countless times. You belong at home."

"But *this* is home!"

"You belong with your family. I've spoken with our bishop and the deacons, too. They agree. Everyone is waiting for your return." His voice grew more insistent with each word.

Naomi cringed. She knew he was going to push the issue ... again. But she didn't realize he'd start in on her from the very first moment he arrived.

"Marvin, I appreciate your concern. Truly, I do." She tried to smile. "But I can't uproot the children again."

"Naomi, it's hardly uprooting them to bring them back home. Back to their family."

She shook her head.

"*Dat's* gone and so is your husband. So, it falls to me to make this decision. I'm your elder brother. You know how this works."

She stepped back, wanting to run away—run away and hide while she still could.

"Don't look so upset," he said. "This is for your good. This is for your children. They need to be raised with family."

"I'm their family," she said, but even she knew how ridiculous that argument was.

"And you'll still be with them." His brow furrowed. "Don't fight me on this, Naomi. We all love you and want you to return."

Panic rumbled through her stomach. He had all the proper arguments on his side. She didn't have anything else to say. Her fists tightened at her sides. She couldn't leave Hollybrook. She just couldn't. She'd grown to love the farm. Besides, she had a business now. She couldn't simply desert it.

She looked around the barn as if searching for an escape. Her eyes settled on the hoe that Zach often carried around as he puttered in her garden when he thought she didn't notice. *Zach.*

Could she leave Zach? Could she?

"Naomi, I plan to take you and the children with me when I leave—"

She tried to interrupt him, but he held up his hand.

"It's settled. I've arranged for a van to pick us up in a week. That'll give us time to pack things up and list the farm to sell."

Naomi's head spun, and she grabbed the doorframe of the barn and held on. She couldn't fathom another change so soon. She couldn't fathom her life being ripped from her again. *No.* She wouldn't do it!

Strength and stubbornness flowed through her, and she drew herself up to her full height. "Marvin, I won't do it. I won't."

His jaw clenched, and his face grew red. "It ain't open to discussion, Naomi. I've said my piece, and that's the way it's going to be. I'll speak with the local bishop if you wish. He'll side with me."

Naomi's bravado was short-lived. He was right. The bishop *would* side with Marvin. Perhaps some of the freer-thinking bishops might disagree, but from what she knew of Bishop Schrock, he wasn't one of them. He'd see Marvin as her authority since both her father and her husband were dead.

She turned on her heel and marched back to the house. She couldn't bear the thought of telling Katy and Ben. Couldn't bear it. Her eyes welled with tears, and she fought the nausea that rose in her throat. A movement to her right caught her attention. She saw Ben running out in the field toward Zachariah, no doubt to tell him that his uncle had arrived.

Ben had grown fond of Zach. More than fond by the looks of things. Her son would be upset to have to leave him. Maybe Katy would be, too. Though she could be as sour as a hen in a rainstorm, Naomi had seen flickers of affection in Katy's eyes for Zach.

She hurried up the porch steps and yanked open the screen. She went into the kitchen to help Katy work on supper. The girl looked up when Naomi entered the room.

"Where's Uncle?" she asked.

"I left him in the barn." Naomi hauled out the big roasting pan from its place on the lower shelf. She plunked it on the counter. "Get the chicken out of the freezer."

"But *Mamm*, it'll never thaw in time."

Naomi stared at Katy. "Get the chicken out of the freezer."

Katy's eyes grew wide at Naomi's curt tone. Without a word, she opened the freezer door and took out the freshly killed and plucked chicken that hadn't been in the freezer more than four days. She carried it to the sink and placed it there. She turned to her mother.

"What's wrong?"

"Nothing," Naomi snapped. "Not a thing. Isn't it nice that Marvin is here to visit?"

She couldn't keep the sarcasm from her voice, and she was ashamed. She wasn't acting in a seemly manner at all. And it wasn't fair of her to burden Katy with her problems. Katy was only a child, after all. There had to be some way out of this. Some way.

She sank to a kitchen chair, twisting a dish towel in her hands. She could go to Bishop Schrock herself and plead her case. Marvin would have to back down if the Bishop gave an opposite decree. Wouldn't he? Naomi knew her brother well. Flexibility wasn't part of his character. Even if Bishop Schrock sided with her, Marvin might still insist she leave. But he could hardly pull her kicking and screaming into the van, could he?

Shame burned through Naomi. What was she thinking? God would be displeased with her behavior *and* her thoughts. A woman was to be submissive. Didn't hundreds of sermons teach her so? She felt her cheeks go hot. What kind of example would she be setting for Katy if she acted with such rebellion? Why, that was how *Englischers* acted, wasn't it?

The ticking of the large round clock over the window reverberated through the kitchen. Naomi saw Katy's lower lip quiver as she turned away and put her attention on unwrapping the chicken. Naomi reached over and took her hand.

"*Ach*, I'm sorry, Katy. Forgive my temper. Everything's all right." Her voice was soft and crooning.

Katy's shoulders relaxed, and she stepped close to lean into Naomi's side. "It's okay, *Mamm*."

"Shall we make a special supper for your uncle? I happen to know that shoo-fly pie is his favorite."

Katy's expression perked up. "I'll make the pie. Can I?"

Naomi chuckled. "Why do you think I mentioned it, our Katy? You make the best pies in the district."

Marvin and Ben came in just before Naomi and Katy set the food on the table. Supper was often a lighter meal in the evening, but that day Naomi and Katy had pulled out all the stops. They served roasted chicken, new potatoes and gravy, green beans, thick slices of homemade bread, and pickles. The crowning glory, of course, was Katy's shoo-fly pie.

After the meal was eaten, Marvin leaned back in the chair and patted his belly. "I'd say that was as good as Ruth's cooking." He gave Katy a wink. "And the best pie I've ever tasted."

Katy blushed and looked at Naomi.

"Marvin, this girl bakes circles around me," Naomi said. She reached over and gave Katy's hand a squeeze.

"We shoulda had Mr. Zach for dinner, too," Ben said.

"*Jah*. About this Zachariah," Marvin began, "he's leasing the land, correct?"

Naomi nodded.

"Ben introduced us." Marvin's keen gaze was on her. "Does he have interest in buying the farm?"

Naomi's eyes widened. Katy plunked her glass back onto the table and the milk inside sloshed dangerously close to the rim.

"Buying the farm?" Katy repeated.

Ben frowned. "Why would *he* buy it? It's ours."

"Why indeed?" Naomi said, giving Marvin a warning glance.

But Marvin was nonplussed. He picked up his mug and took a sip of coffee. "Just wondering," he said.

"*Nee*, he's not interested," Naomi said tersely.

"You asked him?"

She bit her lower lip and shook her head.

"I think that's a mighty good place to start." He set his cup back down. "I'm a bit tired from the journey." He looked at both the children. "Let's meet in the front room for Bible reading and prayer in a few minutes. Then I plan to turn in."

Naomi stood. "Katy, shall we clear the table and *red* up the kitchen."

Katy got up and stumbled after her to the kitchen. "*Mamm?*"

Naomi's expression was pinched. "Let's not worry about anything right now," she said, forcing herself to put a smile on her face. "You wash and I'll dry. How does that sound?"

"But *Mamm*, why would Mr. Zach buy our farm?"

Naomi poured liquid soap into the sink and started the faucet. "It's just an idea your uncle had."

"*Mamm!*" Katy put her hands on her hips. "I'm not a child."

Naomi turned the faucet back off and gazed at her daughter. She studied Katy's indignant look and her proud stance, and alarm coursed through her. Was this the behavior she was instilling in her? This stubborn pride? Was she raising her daughter to be rebellious? She blinked and leaned heavily against the counter. This was no good. No good, at all.

If she allowed her daughter to act like this, where would it lead? How would Katy handle *rumspringa* when she was given a good deal of freedom? This had to be nipped in the bud.

"Don't speak to your elders in such a tone," Naomi corrected her. She drew herself into what she hoped was a stance of authority. "We're not going to discuss this right now."

Katy's mouth tightened, and Naomi saw her work to control her words. Naomi waited, her eyes steady on the girl. Finally, Katy slumped, and her gaze dropped to the floor.

"I'm sorry, *Mamm*," she mumbled.

Naomi felt a part of her heart break as she drew her daughter into her arms. How she wished Isaac was still there. Raising a daughter alone was no small task, and she had no idea if she was doing it correctly. She didn't even have her own mother to rely on for wisdom and advice.

She looked over the top of Katy's head toward the front room where Marvin would be waiting for them with the German Bible open. Maybe he was right. Maybe they should go back to Pennsylvania. She'd have more support there. More help in raising her children. She took a deep breath and pressed her lips together.

Maybe Marvin's arrival was in God's timing. Maybe God was providing for her through her brother.

Naomi was awake hours before dawn broke. She tossed restlessly in her bed, attempting to talk herself into moving back to Pennsylvania. Her mind flitted through the reasons, and there were plenty. Truth be told, when she got down to it, there were few reasons to remain in Hollybrook. Very few.

Her husband and parents were gone. They wouldn't care if she stuck it out in Indiana just because it had been their dream. Isaac would want her to be where it was best for the children. And for her.

So, was Pennsylvania the best for them? She had wept when they'd left, sorry to say good-bye to all her family and friends there. But when they'd arrived to the Hollybrook farm and had moved all their things in, and when she'd seen the complete joy and satisfaction on her husband's face, all her weeping stopped. She'd thrown herself into their new district. She'd made a good friend in Mary. She'd watched her children thrive.

It had been good. So good.

Until the accident. Naomi clutched her hands to her chest. Isaac was torn from her in an instant, and her parents were no more. All the children had left was her. And the farm. Naomi threw the quilt back and rose from her bed. She padded over to the open window and gazed out on the land. She inhaled the sweet smell of growing plants and the aroma of the blossoms bordering the walkway. In the growing light, she watched the leaves on the elm tree dance gently in the morning air. A rooster crowed the day's beginnings.

How could she leave such a beautiful place?

She looked to the left where, if she positioned herself just right, she could observe the barn door. It was open. Zach must be there. She watched, waiting to see his solid form as he went out to the fields. She didn't have to wait long. He paused at the door of the barn and looked toward the house. She ducked back behind the curtains but kept her eyes on him. Even through the shadows, she knew he was watching her window. He wouldn't be able to see her though; it wasn't light enough, and she was mostly hidden.

She would miss him. Tears stung the back of her eyelids, and she knew at that moment that she'd made her decision. She would take the children and go back with Marvin. It was the only sensible thing to do. She wouldn't have to struggle to make ends meet. She wouldn't have to raise her children alone. They would be surrounded by family, by people who loved them.

Zach lowered his head and turned toward the field. For a moment the day before, she had thought Zach had feelings for her. She'd thought he had been upset when she mentioned Marvin's arrival and the reason for his visit. But he hadn't said anything. Hadn't declared any intentions towards her.

She'd hoped he would have. She sucked in her breath. So she *did* have feelings for him? Her heart squeezed beneath her ribs. What difference did it make? He obviously wasn't going to pursue anything with her. She fingered the curtains at the window and took slow even breaths. Yes, she would miss him. She would miss his eyes on her. She would miss his steady presence in her life. She would miss hearing the sound of his laughter when he was with Ben out in the barn.

She turned away from the window. Was she destined to miss people her entire life? Was that what her lot was to be? She would never stop missing Isaac. *Never.* She accepted that. Nor would she ever stop missing her parents. But missing Zach?

That didn't seem necessary.

With a sigh, she dressed for the day. She'd break the news to the children after breakfast. *Dear Gott, please, please, let it go well.*

When the children had run off to do their before-breakfast chores, Marvin took Naomi aside. "Well, sister? Are you ready to start packing?"

Naomi swallowed past the growing knot in her throat. "I need to talk to the children first. You can give me that much time, can't you?" Her voice was short-tempered, and she immediately apologized. "*Ach*, I'm sorry, Marvin. I didn't get much sleep."

He nodded and tugged on the end of his scraggly beard. "Understandable. I thought I'd approach Zachariah about purchasing the farm."

"*Nee!*" Naomi interjected. "Please let me do it."

"I will do it for you."

"*Nee.* I've been handling all the business up till now. Let me do this." She felt her cheeks go hot. She was disgusted with herself, for she well knew the reason she wanted to be the one to approach Zach. She wanted to watch his face, hear his tone of voice. She wanted to discern whether there was any emotion there for her.

Of anyone in the district, it would be most fitting if Zach bought the farm. He knew it better than anyone. Better than she did. Better even than her husband and her parents. He'd worked the land longer.

"All right, Naomi. But I'm right here to finish up the business."

"*Jah.* Thank you."

She turned to put breakfast on the table. The children would be back any minute, and she didn't want to put off the inevitable for a moment longer than necessary. Perhaps, when everyone knew, she could adjust to the idea with more grace and eagerness herself.

Because right then, all she felt was dread.

The children bounded in the side door, washed up, and took their seats at the table. This time, Marvin led the silent grace.

Chapter Four

After eating, Katy stood to begin clearing the table. "Wait a moment, Katy," Naomi said, reaching out and touching her arm. "I want to talk with both you children."

Marvin rose. "I'll leave you to it," he said. "I'll be out on the porch should you need me."

Both Ben's and Katy's face reflected their curiosity.

"What's going on?" Katy asked, hesitation in her tone.

Naomi licked her lips. "Children, Marvin didn't only come to visit us," she began. "He and the rest of the family..." She looked at her children and gave them a smile, albeit somewhat forced. "You remember all your aunts and uncles and cousins. Well, they are really missing us—"

"They shoulda come with Uncle then," Ben said with a big grin. "I coulda showed 'em all my frogs and stuff."

"It would have been too difficult and expensive for all of them to make the trip. So they sent Marvin as a kind of representative."

Katy frowned. "Representative? I don't understand."

"The family wants us to move back to Pennsylvania." Naomi held her breath, bracing herself for their reaction.

To her surprise, they said nothing. They both simply stared at her, their mouths open.

"Did you hear me?" she asked.

"But we live here now," Ben said, scratching his arm.

"What about Liz?" Katy asked, her mind immediately going to her best friend. "I wouldn't ever get to see her anymore."

Naomi cleared her throat. "You can write each other. Wouldn't it be fun to get letters all the time? I know how excited you are when we hear from our family in Pennsylvania."

"Letters?" Katy asked, her voice rising. "You can't play with letters!"

Naomi sighed and clasped her hands firmly in her lap. "*Nee.* You can't." She gave Katy a sympathetic look. "But Marvin and the family think it's for the best. You'll have all your cousins and your aunts and uncles. And remember your old friends? They're still there."

"What about Mr. Zach?" Ben asked. "Is he gonna come with us?"

"Don't be stupid," Katy snapped.

"Katy Byler! That's enough of that," Naomi scolded. She looked at Ben. "*Nee*, son. Mr. King's family is here. He won't be coming with us."

Ben's wide eyes welled with tears. "But who's gonna play with me? Who's gonna teach me stuff."

Naomi felt as if she'd been slapped. She gulped air and composed her face. "Your uncles, Ben. And your cousins. They love you and are eager to be with you."

Katy's lower lip quivered, and she reached across the table and touched Ben's arm. "I'll teach you stuff," she said, and her voice cracked.

Naomi was startled by her daughter's tender gesture. Maybe this wouldn't be so bad after all.

"Can I be excused now?" Katy asked. Her voice was wooden. She leveled a shadowed look at her mother, her demeanor resigned.

"*Jah*."

"I don't wanna go," Ben said, his tears starting to fall. "Does Mr. Zach know? He never told me."

"*Nee*. He doesn't know. I'm going to tell him in a few minutes."

"I don't wanna go. I like it here."

Naomi blew out her breath. "So do I, Ben. But we like Pennsylvania, too. Everything's going to be all right. You'll see."

Ben wiped at the tears on his cheeks. "I don't wanna go," he repeated and dropped his head on his arms.

Naomi stood and kissed the top of his head. "Right now, why don't you go out to Marvin on the porch? He'd love to visit with you a bit."

Ben climbed off the long bench and shuffled over to the front door. Naomi wanted to call him back and tell him that they weren't going after all. She wanted to laugh and tell him it wasn't true, that they were staying in Hollybrook.

Instead, she squared her shoulders and went into the washroom and through the side door. Outside, she shaded her eyes with her hand, scanning the fields. And then she saw him. He was in the far corner of the field. She took off toward him, her heart squeezing painfully with each step.

"Naomi!" Zach cried when he saw her approaching. "What's wrong?"

She never walked out to the fields to find him, so it only made sense that he would be alarmed.

"Are the *kinner* all right?" He strode towards her.

She held up her hand. "They're fine, Zach."

He stopped before her, and his brows were drawn with concern. "Your brother? He's all right?"

She nodded, a lump growing in her throat. "He's fine."

"Then what is it?"

"Do you want to buy the farm?" she blurted.

He gaped at her and took a half step back. "What?"

"Do you want to buy the farm?" she repeated, blinking rapidly, trying to keep the impending tears from falling.

"You're selling it?" he said, his eyes searching hers.

She nodded.

He took off his straw hat and held it, his fingers circling the brim. "I don't understand."

"We're going back to Pennsylvania with Marvin." She watched him, hoping, no praying, that he would say something, anything, to make her stay.

"I see."

Her heart sank, and she swallowed hard.

He licked his lips. "What about your Bed and Breakfast."

She shrugged. "It will close, I guess. It won't matter that much. I only barely got started with it."

"But I thought you liked it."

"I do."

He put his hat back on, pushing it down on his head. The brim shadowed his face, and she wanted to step closer to look into his eyes, but she didn't dare.

"You didn't answer me," she said. "About buying the farm, I mean."

He exhaled. "Naomi, I don't have that kind of money right now."

"How do you know? I haven't told you what it costs. I won't cheat you. I only need to get out from under the debt." She was talking fast, realizing she knew next to nothing about selling land.

He stepped closer. She could see his eyes now, and they looked dark and angry.

"I would never think you'd cheat me," he said, his voice clipped. "How could you believe so little of me?"

She blanched. What? She didn't believe little of him. Why was he so angry? She'd only been explaining that the price wouldn't be inflated.

"I-I'm sorry, Mr. King." She stared at him.

"*Mr. King?*" He turned to the side and spit on the ground. Instinctively, she backed up, confused by his behavior. He was hotly angry now, and she wasn't sure why.

"My brother will talk to you about it then," she finally said.

He glared at her and turned on his heel and walked away. She shook her head. What had just happened? He stopped and turned back to her.

"When are you leaving?" he asked, over-enunciating every word.

"A week."

He hit his hand on his thigh. "Of course."

She turned and fled, running through the field, brushing against the corn and feeling it tug at her dress. What was the *matter* with him? She'd thought that he would at least voice a bit of sorrow at her leaving. As she ran, her mouth tightened. He was crazy, that man. And heartless. She wanted to turn and yell *Good Riddance!* at him, but she wouldn't be so crude.

When she rounded the corner of the big house, she stopped short. A blue car with rust running around the bottom of the doors, was parked before the porch. A woman with two young children stood on the first step. Marvin was talking to her.

"Hello?" Naomi said, approaching the woman.

She turned and Naomi gave a start at how beautiful she was. Liquid blue eyes sparkled, and her left cheek dimpled with an eager smile.

"They told me at the Feed and Supply that you have a Bed and Breakfast. I'm looking for a place to stay for a few nights."

Marvin caught Naomi's eye. "I told her that you're closed for business."

Naomi bristled. She had one more week. She didn't need to close yet. She gave her brother a look of apology and turned to the woman. "My brother's right. We'll be closing soon. But I do believe that we can help you for a couple nights at least."

She heard her brother sputter, but she kept her eyes on the woman, who broke out into an even greater smile at her words.

"That's wonderful! And don't worry. My children behave well. This here is Daisy, and that's John."

Naomi laughed. "I never gave it a thought. Nice to meet you, children. Come. You can stay in the *daadi haus*."

"Let's go, kids," the woman said, her voice light and airy. "Let's go to the *daadi haus*."

Something in the way she said *daadi haus* made Naomi suspect that she was familiar with the term.

"So, you know what a *daadi haus* is?" Naomi asked.

The woman's face flushed. "Yes. Yes, I do."

But she didn't say anything further, and Naomi didn't want to pry. She opened the door to the small house and ushered the woman and her children inside.

"You can sleep in the main bedroom, and your children can each have a single bed in here." Naomi noted that Katy had done a fine job of cleaning the day before. It looked nice and tidy. "If you'd like to take meals with us, we'll eat dinner at noon and supper at six o'clock."

"That would be right nice," the woman said. "When would you like me to pay?"

"You can pay now or when you leave." Naomi told her the price, and the woman nodded. "I should get your name," Naomi added.

The woman faced her, and a look of dread flashed over her face so quickly Naomi wasn't sure she'd seen it. "The name is Marcy," she said, her voice dipping. "Marcy Blackenship."

Naomi almost choked. *Marcy Blackenship?* Wasn't that the name of Zach's old girlfriend? She stared at the woman in shock and then quickly worked to recover her senses. "U-uh, hello Marcy. I'm Naomi."

No wonder the woman knew what a *daadi haus* was. *She'd been Amish.*

"Nice to meet you, Naomi."

"I'll leave you to get settled," Naomi said, grateful that her voice sounded normal. "Let me know if you need anything."

"We will."

Naomi stumbled out of the house. Did Zach know Marcy was coming? And did he know that she would be staying there with *her*? Naomi shuddered and wondered what it all meant. But she knew before anything else, she'd have to go and deal with her brother's anger. He wouldn't take kindly to her countering his wishes in public like that.

And she was right. He stood on the porch waiting for her, and his angry scowl was one she remembered well from childhood.

"Naomi..."

She rushed up the steps. "Before you get mad at me, let me speak. I know you don't want me to take guests, but they'll be my last ones. I like the Bed and Breakfast. I'm going to miss it when we leave. So can't you at least let me have these last two nights? And besides, we can use the money to help pay for gas for the trip back to Pennsylvania."

She spoke quickly and with passion, trying to ignore the confusion that thundered through her regarding the identity of her guest. Hadn't Marcy used her maiden surname? Wouldn't that mean she had never married, even though she had two children? What was Zach going to do?

Marvin looked at her and much to Naomi's surprise, his expression softened. "All right, Naomi. I understand what you're saying. Have your three guests. But remember, you have to be ready in a week to leave."

"How can I take everything with me in a week? And in a van, no less? The way I see it, all we can really take is our clothes and perhaps a few things we hold dear. But I won't leave the quilts behind. Nor *Mamm's* favorite dishes."

He touched her shoulder. "I can arrange for a truck to bring the furniture at a later date."

Naomi shook her head. "*Nee.*"

"What do you mean?"

"I assume we'll live in someone's *daadi haus*, right? And they'll already have it furnished. We might as well leave most everything here." Grief tore up her throat then, and she couldn't stand there pretending to be fine for another minute. She rushed into the house and up to her room where she fell on her bed and sobbed. Sobbed for another tearing loss in her life. Sobbed for her children. Sobbed for her dead husband and parents. Sobbed for her growing affection for Zach that was never to be.

Chapter Five

Marcy and her two children spent part of the afternoon lollygagging about on the front porch. Naomi could hardly take her eyes from them, especially Marcy. She studied her, wanting to know the draw she had on Zachariah. There were her looks, of course, but Naomi instinctively knew that looks alone wouldn't be enough for Zach. There had to be something in Marcy's personality that had dazzled him.

Zach hadn't come in from the fields yet, and she wondered whether she should go out and warn him. Unless he already knew, of course. But surely, he would have told her if he'd known Marcy was coming. Naomi stepped back from the window, embarrassed to be spending so much time spying on a guest. The house was quiet. She had no idea where Marvin was, and Ben had holed himself up in his room and wouldn't come out. Katy had run off to Liz's house, no doubt to share her upsetting news regarding the move.

She leaned her hands on the kitchen counter and closed her eyes. Zach would want to know. As a friend, she needed to tell him. Part of her wanted to, for she wanted to note his reaction. Another part of her was afraid to tell him. And for the same reason. What if he became full of glee at the news? What then?

Of course, it didn't matter. She was leaving.

She wiped her damp hands on a dishtowel and slipped out the side door to go out to the fields. She hoped Marvin wasn't around to observe her. She knew he wouldn't approve of her traipsing off to talk to Zach. Well, she was going to do it. She owed Zach as much.

Zach was in the middle of the fields, pulling back a tassel to inspect the cob beneath when she approached.

"Naomi? Again?" He dropped his hands and beheld her. "What is it this time?" There was an edge to his voice, and she stiffened.

"I want to tell you something."

"*Jah?* What is it?"

"Marcy's here." The two words might as well have been well-aimed arrows for the effect they had on Zach. He flinched, and his face went white. He stepped back, nearly trampling on the corn stalks. "What?"

"She's here. Staying at my Bed and Breakfast."

"*What?*" His voice was frantic, and he shook his head as if trying to wrap his mind around her news.

"She's here with her two children. I don't know why. I imagine she's looking for you."

He gaped at her, and she saw his jaw clench.

She continued. "She doesn't have any family around here anymore, does she?"

He shook his head, and she saw him swallow. Hard.

"Did she ask for me?" The words scraped up his throat.

"*Nee.*"

He looked over the tops of the corn toward the house. Naomi followed his gaze, although she wasn't tall enough to see the house clearly. With stiff movements, he went back to pulling back random tassels.

"You're not going to go see her?" Naomi asked, incredulous.

He ignored her, continuing about his business. To a casual observer, it might look like nothing was amiss. But Naomi knew better. His face was set, harder than usual. And his hands shook ever so slightly.

He was disturbed. Deeply disturbed.

"Zach?" she whispered.

Again, he ignored her. She sighed heavily and turned to go. Without looking back, she knew his eyes were on her, watching her every move as she left the field to go back to the house.

Approaching Marcy on the front porch, she smiled. "Would you like some cool lemonade?"

"That'd be right nice," Marcy said, tossing her shiny brown hair over her shoulder.

"*Gut*. Children, I'll get each of you a glass, too." The two children, both as attractive as their mother, grinned. "And after your drink, you can play in the tire swing if you like."

"Can we, Mom?" asked Daisy, her eyes dancing.

"Of course," Marcy agreed.

Naomi went inside and poured lemonade into four glasses. She decided that she'd sit a spell with Marcy, get to know her a bit. Going back outside, she served the three of them and then took a glass for herself, sitting in a free rocker. The two children gulped down their drinks and raced off toward the tire swing.

Naomi smiled at Marcy. "I hope you enjoy your stay in Hollybrook," she said.

Marcy put both hands around her glass, as if absorbing its coolness. "I'm sure we will. I've been here before, you know."

NAOMI'S CHOICE

"Oh?"

"You're new, aren't you?"

"I've been here over a year."

"I used to live in Hollybrook myself." Marcy blinked, and her smile was sad. "I was a right mess. We had to leave sudden-like." She gazed out at the yard, her eyes lost in her memories. "I made the biggest mistakes of my life here." She gave a quick laugh. "Oh, most folks would say that having my children was my biggest mistake. Or my biggest sin. But look at them." She glanced over her shoulder toward the playing children. "They're beautiful. They're something I did right."

Naomi was shocked that this woman would talk so freely to her. They didn't know each other.

"I was engaged once. I let him go."

Naomi stiffened. She wondered how anyone could let Zachariah King go. He was such a fine man, and she knew he had been equally as fine all those years ago. Men like Zachariah didn't change. They remained steadfast and true.

"Perhaps you know him," Marcy said, her expression eager. "Zach King."

Naomi inhaled deeply. "Mr. King leases my land."

Marcy gave such a start, she nearly dropped her glass. The lemonade sloshed and some dribbled down the side of the glass. "What?"

"He's in the fields right now." Naomi wondered whether she should have divulged such information, but she could hardly stay quiet about it, could she? That would look like she was hiding something.

"Zachariah?" Marcy said with a gasp. "He's here? Right now?"

Naomi nodded, and her stomach felt as if a crate of cement blocks had been placed on it. There was no mistaking the look of love and joy on Marcy's face.

Marcy set down her glass and jolted up from her chair. "Where?"

Naomi rose and gestured for Marcy to follow her. She led her to the edge of the field and pointed. Marcy gave Naomi's arm a quick squeeze and ran off through the fields. Naomi couldn't bear to watch her. She turned and moved back to the porch, just in time to see her friend Mary come up the drive in her pony cart.

"Naomi!" she cried as she neared her. "Naomi!"

Naomi raised her hand in greeting and worked to keep her tears from falling. "Hello, Mary."

Mary reined in her horse and climbed out of the cart. "What's this I hear?"

Naomi looked into the dear face of her friend and burst into tears.

"*Ach*! Naomi! So, it's true! You *are* leaving!" She grabbed Naomi's arm and led her up the stairs to the porch. "Sit down. Tell me."

Naomi sank into a rocker and buried her face in her hands. Everything was wrong. She'd thought that nothing could ever happen that was worse than the accident. In that, she'd been right. But she'd never thought that horrible things would continue to happen to her, continue to darken her path. Just when she'd gathered hope that maybe life could be good again, Marvin had to come and dash all her dreams. And now, Marcy's presence was killing any hope she had with Zach.

The hard truth was that Naomi would never be able to see anything through at the farm. She'd never be able to see if there could be a good life for her there in Hollybrook.

And she would lose Zach.

And her friend, Mary.

Mary crooned over her, patting her back. "Tell me about it. You're really leaving then? My Jack said he met your brother at the Feed and Supply. They got to talking, and your brother said you're going back to Pennsylvania. Why, Naomi? I thought you liked it here."

"I do," Naomi cried. "I don't want to go." She wiped her tears and looked up at Mary. "Marvin is insisting. And he's right, you know. Back in Pennsylvania, I'd have help with the children. I wouldn't have to worry about making money every minute of the day."

Mary grimaced and plopped into the rocker beside Naomi. "What's changed? It's been this way since your husband died. What's changed now?"

Naomi pressed her lips together, not wanting to consider Mary's question, because nothing had really changed. She was still tired. She was still weary of worrying about money. But she had the Bed and Breakfast now. And she had Zach. She gave a sharp intake of breath. No, she didn't. She didn't have Zach at all. *Marcy did.*

Mary looked at the car in the drive. "You have guests?"

"Marcy Blackenship and her two kids."

Mary's mouth dropped open, and she grabbed Naomi's shoulder. "Marcy? She's here?"

Naomi nodded miserably. "She's in the fields with Zach."

"What?"

"She went racing out there as soon as I told her where he was."

"Nee!" Mary's eyes stretched wide, and she covered her mouth with her hand.

"He didn't know she was coming. But when I told him she was here, I saw his reaction. He's not over her, Mary."

Mary studied her face. "And that bothers you?"

Naomi looked away and didn't answer.

"Naomi!" Mary said. "Look at me."

With reluctance, Naomi turned back to her friend.

"You love him."

Did she? Did she *love* him? It didn't matter.

"He doesn't love me." Naomi wanted to sink into the earth and disappear forever. She chided herself. What a ridiculous thing to wish for. She was a mother, after all, and she had wonderful people in her life. *Forgive me, dear Father in Heaven.*

"Naomi Byler, haven't I been telling you for weeks that Zach has feelings for you? Haven't I? I've known that man since we were both knee-high to a grasshopper. He has feelings for you, for sure and for certain."

Naomi shook her head over and over.

Mary put her hand on Naomi's lap. "He's shy is all."

"Doesn't matter anymore, anyway." Naomi blinked away her tears. "Marcy's here now."

Mary twisted around. "Those her kids?"

"*Jah*. They're lovely, aren't they?"

Mary shrugged. "So are yours."

"Oh, Mary. This isn't a competition. And if it was, Marcy would be the victor. Who knows what's going on right now in the field?"

"Pretty brazen for her to rush off like that, chasing a man."

Naomi's cheeks went hot. Hadn't she run off to the field to see Zach herself? And more than once.

"I don't want you to move." Mary puckered her lips into a pout. "You've become my closest friend, Naomi Byler. Just writing each other won't be the same."

"*Nee*, it won't."

Mary stood up and shook out her apron. "Shame on me. The Lord God is in control. It isn't up to us to question His ways. He knows what's what."

Naomi smiled. Only Mary would phrase it like that.

"I'll come again tomorrow," she said crisply. "You'll need help with your packing."

"Thank you, Mary."

She waved away Naomi's gratitude. "I'll be here after the noon meal." And with that, she climbed back into her pony cart, gave a snap to the reins, and was off.

Naomi closed her eyes and breathed in the moist summer air. She would miss her friend. Mary had helped her recover from her grief. Mary had given her moments of laughter when she'd thought she would never laugh again. Mary had made life bearable and time after time had assured her that all would be well.

Daisy ran up the steps of the porch, startling Naomi out of her thoughts.

"Where's my mom?" she asked.

"She's on a walk in the fields. She'll be back soon," Naomi said.

She heard Marcy's voice coming around the corner of the house. And Zach's voice. Naomi shot out of her chair and faced them. Marcy's face was red and glistening with perspiration. Naomi wondered at that as it wasn't terribly hot. When he saw Naomi, Zach clammed up completely, closing his lips into a tight line. Naomi tried to read the look in his eyes, but all she saw was turmoil.

She bit her lip until it throbbed like her pulse. There could be only one reason for such turmoil in Zach's eyes. He still loved Marcy. Her anguish grew until she had to fight to keep her composure.

"Naomi, I didn't know you were still out here," Marcy said, blinking and wiping the top of her lip.

Daisy pulled on her mother's arm. "Mom, John and I are hungry. Can we eat some of our snacks?"

Marcy flinched as if she'd forgotten she even had a daughter. "What? Oh. Yes, of course. Go ahead."

"Come on, John!" hollered Daisy. "She said yes!"

The two scampered around to the *daadi haus*.

Zach's face had gone dark, and Naomi could see that she was in the way. "I have work to do," she mumbled and fairly ran into the house.

The screen slammed behind her, and she shut the door, too, leaning against it and breathing hard. What were they saying out there? Did Marcy want to become Amish again? To ask forgiveness, to obey whatever the bishop decreed, and be welcomed back? And how would Daisy and John like that? Were they willing to embrace their mother's roots?

She sank down to the floor and rested her chin on her knees. She closed her eyes. *Don't do it, Zach. Don't do it.* With a start, she realized what she was chanting, and she shivered. It wasn't her concern. How wrong of her to impose herself into Zach's business. Into *God's* business.

She put her arms around her legs and tried to talk herself into getting up and getting about her work. If they were to move in a few days, she needed to begin packing. Most importantly, she needed to go through all their things, decide what she had room to take and what had to be left.

Would Zach buy the farm? He hadn't really responded to her.

She hoped he would. He loved the farm. That was evident in the way he cared for it, always puttering around after his work in the fields, fixing things and watching over things that had nothing to do with leasing the land.

She rose and couldn't help but glance out her window. Zach and Marcy were standing close, talking, their faces intent, as if no one else in the world existed. Naomi sighed and felt a sense of loss—an emotion that sat on her with unwanted familiarity. She quivered, and tried to shrug it off, but it had sunk its fingers into her once again.

She squared her shoulders and walked to the kitchen. *Mamm's* favorite dishes would have to be packed. They comforted Naomi; their pattern of small yellow flowers around the edge brought her cheer even on her darkest days. Using them was like having her mother still with her, and she couldn't help but think *Mamm* would be pleased. Someday, Naomi would hand the dishes down to Katy, who would use them with equal pleasure.

Yes, the dishes had to come. And what about *Dat's* tools? They should be kept for Ben. Perhaps not all of the tools, for they would fill boxes and boxes. The special tools. Naomi smiled to herself. What made a tool special? Maybe she should let Ben choose.

There was a knock at the door, and Naomi's attention was jerked back to Zach and Marcy. She hurried to answer it, wondering which one of them would be there. It was Zach. He gave her a guarded look and for a moment said nothing.

"*Jah?*" Naomi asked, hardly daring to breathe. When he didn't say anything, she grew worried and aggravated. He was the one who knocked on the door. Did he expect her to start the conversation?

"Naomi?" He licked his lips. "You all right?"

What an absurd question. Of course, she was all right. She frowned and wondered what he was getting at.

"Marcy's leaving."

"*What?*" Relief roared through her.

"Marcy's leaving."

"Why are *you* the one telling me?"

"She asked me to."

"So she's not even staying the night?"

"*Nee.*"

The relief multiplied and expanded and filled her every cell. If Marcy was leaving, didn't that mean... Zach stepped back from the door and pushed his straw hat back onto his head. He gave her a curt nod and turned away.

"Wait," she burst out.

He stopped but didn't look back at her.

"Are *you* all right?"

He didn't answer. He raised his hand in a backward wave and tromped down the steps and back toward the field. Naomi's eyebrows rose. What had happened between him and Marcy?

Within minutes, Daisy and John came around the house, lugging their bags. Daisy dropped hers with a thud and opened the trunk. They both threw their bags inside, but Daisy wasn't tall enough to grab it shut again. Naomi went down the steps toward them.

"Need some help?"

"I can't reach it. You just gotta slam it."

Naomi easily reached the trunk and slammed it shut. She shook her head, realizing it was the first time in her life that she'd shut the trunk of a car. Whenever she rode in a van, the driver handled such things. Vans didn't have trunks, anyway. Considering the emotion of the moment, Naomi marveled that she could be pondering such mundane things as car trunks.

Marcy walked toward the van, and Naomi could see her eyes were red and swollen. Even after a crying jag, the girl looked beautiful. A tinge of jealousy threaded through Naomi. She hurried toward Marcy and took her bag from her.

"Let me," she said.

Marcy blew out her breath. "I'm sorry for the change of plans."

"That's fine."

"I can pay you for the time we were here."

Naomi shook her head. "Don't be silly. It was nothing. Can I get you a snack for your journey? Would the children like some cookies?"

John jumped out of the backseat. "Can we, Mom?"

Daisy planted herself in the passenger seat in front and folded her arms across her chest. Her lips pressed into a tight pucker, and she didn't look willing to budge.

"I suppose so," Marcy said, her voice trailing. Then she looked at John. "I'll go get them. You get back in the car."

Naomi handed Marcy's bag to John. Then she took Marcy into the house. She heard her sniffing behind her as they entered the kitchen. Naomi got out a paper bag and a couple paper napkins. She lined the sack and then began placing cookies inside. By then, Marcy had begun to weep, and Naomi couldn't simply pretend that she wasn't. She set the sack on the counter and led Marcy to her kitchen bench.

"Sit down for a minute," she said. "Would you like some water? Or tea?"

Marcy shook her head and put her hands to her face. "I'm sorry," she muttered through her fingers. "I'm a mess."

Naomi sat beside her.

"Zach said..." A fresh bout of tears began. "Zach said that he..." Marcy couldn't continue. She merely sobbed into her hands.

Naomi waited, feeling awful for her pain.

After a minute or two, Marcy got ahold of herself. "I'm sorry." She removed her hands from her face. Naomi handed her a napkin, and Marcy dabbed at her eyes and blew her nose. "I left the Amish." She gazed at Naomi with wide eyes.

Naomi nodded. "I know."

"I don't really regret it." She looked at Naomi as if gauging her reaction. "Too many rules for me. No freedom at all."

Naomi bristled at her words but chose to let it go.

"I was a wild teen. Didn't want to listen to anyone. Least of all my parents or the bishop. Heaven forbid that I listen to *him*!" She gave a wry laugh. "I was insufferable. Finally, in total humiliation, my parents left the area, and I went with them. Sort of. I ran around a lot." She dropped her hands to her lap and got a faraway look in her eyes.

"Zach was my beau. He loved me." She glanced at Naomi. "He loved me with his whole heart. He tried to talk sense into me, but I wouldn't listen to him either. Even though I knew how much he loved me, I just couldn't do it. I couldn't be the proper little Amish girl. I'd tasted my freedom by then, and oh, how sweet it was."

Naomi watched the emotions play over her face. She watched her delicate brow furrow, her rosy lips part. She saw Marcy as Zach might have seen her, and she understood his broken heart.

"Things in my life lately ... uh, things have been difficult." Her eyes teared up again. "My parents are both gone, and I wanted a family again." She bit her lips. "I stupidly thought I might be able to come home to Hollybrook. But I couldn't. I thought that Zach—"

She stopped abruptly and gasped, grabbing Naomi's hand. Her eyes grew huge as she stared at Naomi. "Oh! I'm so blind!" She shook her head, and her lips parted. "I'm such a fool, sitting here going on and on about Zach and me. I didn't even think. I didn't realize..."

Naomi felt Marcy's grip on her hand tighten. She wanted to pull away from this beautiful girl. She wasn't accustomed to such familiarity with a stranger. But she didn't know how to extricate herself without causing a scene.

Marcy stared at her. "It's *you*, isn't it?"

Naomi blanched. "*Me?* I'm sorry. I don't know what—"

"He's fallen for *you*!"

Naomi did pull her hand away then. She got up and went back to the cookies, putting two more into the sack with shaking hands. "You're cookies are ready," she said, turning and offering the bag to Marcy.

Marcy shook her head. "I get it. I was Amish for years. These things aren't spoken about. Well, I'm *Englisch* now. A *fancy* girl. So I can speak as I wish. Zach would hardly listen to me. Oh, he stood there all right, and I saw the pain in his eyes. He's still not over me, but he won't take me back. Lord! I was even willing to play Amish with him." She shook her head and reached out to take the bag of cookies. "Letting him go is the one regret I have. But at the time, I couldn't have Zach *and* my new freedom. I tried more than once. You know, coming back, going to Sunday meeting. It about killed me."

She got up and stepped close to Naomi, staring deeply into her eyes. "You're a good woman. I can see that. I wish you well."

Without a further word, she turned on her heel and left, her hips gently swaying in her snug jeans. Naomi watched her go, emotions tumbling through her heart.

Despite the girl's frankness, despite her brazenness, Naomi liked her. Marcy Blackenship had an appeal, a careless magnetism that drew a person. Naomi peered through the kitchen window and saw her car disappear down the drive. She wished her well, too.

Somehow, she knew Marcy would land on her feet.

Chapter Six

If Naomi thought that once Marcy left, Zach would make a move in their relationship, she was dead wrong. During the next day and a half, she didn't see him. She wasn't even sure he came to work in the fields. She was too busy in the house, packing and sorting.

"Did Zach King give you an answer yet?" Marvin asked her on the third day. "I've spoken with some realtors, but until we have an answer from Zach, I don't feel right about listing it."

"Listing it?"

"The farm. With the realtors. I think it only fair that Zach get first chance."

"He hasn't answered me." Naomi hated to admit it, but she was hurt. Zach hadn't even come around to ask how the packing was going. Nor had he come around to check on Ben and how he was faring with the prospect of moving, and the two of them were close. "You can ask Zach yourself, Marvin."

"Perhaps he's been getting the finances he needs to buy the place." Marvin looked down at the box Naomi was filling with knickknacks from the front room. "You taking that stuff?"

Naomi paused, her hands falling to her sides. "You don't think I should?"

He shrugged. "Doesn't look too important to me."

Inwardly, Naomi balked. Since he was forcing this move on her, the least he could do was be more supportive. He must have noticed her reaction. "Ah, don't listen to me, Naomi. If Ruth was here, she'd scold me for being cold-hearted."

Naomi smiled. She liked her sister-in-law. In truth, it *would* be nice to see her again. "Ruth would be right."

Marvin laughed. "Is Zach out in the fields today?"

"I haven't seen him."

"Well, if you do, tell him I need to talk with him."

So do I, she thought. But since Marcy's leaving, Zach had seemed to disappear right along with her.

Marvin wandered off, and Naomi stood up. She straightened to her full height and decided that she was going to get an answer from Zach once and for all. He either wanted the farm or he didn't. This silly business of ignoring her question had gone too far.

She tossed down her apron and marched out to the barn to hitch up the pony cart. She'd go to Zach's home herself. Granted, it wasn't the normal course of action for an Amish woman. In fact, Mary would scold her heartily if she knew what Naomi was doing. But right then, Naomi didn't care. She'd be leaving the district soon, anyway, so what did it matter now?

She hollered to Marvin to please watch the children, and she didn't wait until he had a chance to question her. Marvin would have a fit, too, if he knew what she was planning to do. She quickly got about the business of hitching up Myrtle. The faster she got the horse hitched up, the faster she could leave.

Since Isaac's passing, Naomi had gotten a lot of practice with hitching up a horse, and it did her in good stead right then. Within minutes,

Myrtle was secure to the pony cart, and she was trotting down the drive and out to the road. Naomi ignored her misgivings about her mission. She knew Zach lived with his folks, and she prayed that they wouldn't be the ones to answer the door.

Within fifteen minutes, she'd arrived. She'd never been to the King farm before, and she wasn't sure whether Zach lived in the main house or the *daadi haus*. Her bravado had completely faded, and she suddenly felt foolish and just plain *wrong* to be approaching either one of the houses. Then she spotted an outbuilding whose door was open. Perhaps if she wondered that direction, she'd meet Zach without having to go to the front door at all.

She slipped down from the cart and cautiously approached the open door. Inside was a wood-working shed. Piles of sawdust lay on the floor, and she heard the scraping sounds of what she thought might be a chisel or a planer. She peeked further inside and saw Zach bent over a board, his hair hanging in tendrils over his forehead and a look of complete concentration on his face. She stood a moment and watched him. Admiration for him burned in her chest. He was such a fine person. She hated that he'd been hurt again with Marcy's return, for she knew without asking that it *had* hurt him. But he'd rejected Marcy. And that had to have been a victory for him, no matter how painful.

She leaned her head against the wooden doorframe and watched the muscles in his arms ripple as he hammered the chisel into the wood. What was he making, anyway? She couldn't see it clearly from her vantage point.

Zach must have felt her presence for he abruptly looked up. When he saw her, he dropped both the chisel and the hammer. He stared at her.

She flushed. "Zach. I'm sorry. I didn't mean to startle you."

He stepped quickly in front of what he was working on, as if to hide it. "What are you doing here?"

She winced at his curt tone. Wasn't he happy to see her at all? "I-I, well, I need an answer from you."

"About the purchase?"

"*Jah*." She held her breath. Her heart raced as she stared at his dark expression. Was he angry?

He didn't move.

"U-uh," she stuttered. "You haven't been around the last couple days. I was worried."

He nodded, a small almost imperceptible movement. "No need to worry."

She took one step forward. "Still. I *did* worry."

His eyes clung to hers, analyzing her, assessing her. She squirmed under his gaze, wondering what he was thinking. What he was hiding on the work table behind him.

She took another step closer. Couldn't he see the love she had for him? Couldn't he sense her longing for him? For his touch, however brief?

Still, he didn't move.

"What are you working on?" she asked. Somehow, she knew that whatever was hidden behind his back was somehow vital to her. And to him.

Another step. His eyes searched her face, reaching into her thoughts.

"Can I see?" she asked, tilting her head toward the space behind him.

Without taking his eyes from hers, he moved aside.

There on the table was a sign. A beautiful, carved sign. She immediately saw the words *Bed and Breakfast* in bold thick letters. But the spot where the word *Byler's* had been carved was sanded over. She moved closer, bending over the wood. *Byler's* was mostly gone, and in its place the word *King's* appeared. It wasn't finished, and right then, it looked a bit of a mess, but she could clearly see what he was doing.

She jolted back, as if she'd been punched. He was going to take over *her* Bed and Breakfast! He planned not only to buy her farm but *to take her business?* She clasped her heart and nearly doubled over from the realization. He could hardly wait till she was gone before he swooped in and took it all.

She gulped hard, and tears flooded her eyes. "You-you—" she choked out, but couldn't continue.

"Naomi?" He moved to her and reached out for her arm. "Naomi?"

She jerked back, harder. "You're taking my Bed and Breakfast?" She stared at him with raging accusation in her eyes. She didn't even know why she was so upset. She was leaving. She'd offered him the farm. What difference did it make if he continued with the Bed and Breakfast, too?

She turned and fled from the shop. Blindly, she clambered into the pony cart and snapped the reins.

"Naomi!" he cried behind her.

Wildly, she hollered at Myrtle to get going. They hadn't gone more than a yard or two, when Zach caught up and reached into the cart, grabbing the reins from her hands and yanking back. Myrtle snorted and stopped short.

"Naomi? What are you doing?"

"Getting out of here! Getting away from you!"

Through her tears, she saw the shock and pain on his face. He shook his head, his mouth open and his face flushed. "Naomi?"

"Quit saying my name! You want it all, don't you! My farm *and* my business!"

She was mortified at herself. She was not making a lick of sense. He wasn't taking anything from her. She had offered the farm to him, and she was leaving.

"*Nee. Nee.*" He shook his head and desperation was on his face. "You don't understand!"

"I understand just fine!" she cried. "You don't even care that I'm leaving!"

He dropped the reins then and grabbed her face with his calloused hands. Without any hesitation at all, he leaned in and pressed his lips to hers. His kiss sent the pit of her stomach into a wild shocked swirl. Stunned, she pushed back, gasping. *"What are you doing?"*

"Don't you understand? Haven't I made myself clear?"

"What?" she cried. *"Made yourself clear?"* All you've made clear is that you don't care a fig that I'm leaving! All you've made clear is that you're angry at me for some reason!" She took a great heaving breath and glared holes through him.

He shook his head. "Naomi, Naomi."

"Quit saying my name!" The man was stark raving mad.

"I *won't* quit saying your name. I won't." He touched her cheek, brushing the back of his hand against it in a gesture so tender, so sweetly gentle, that Naomi burst into tears.

"Ah, Naomi," he whispered. "I want you to marry me. Don't you see? The Bed and Breakfast would become *King's* Bed and Breakfast. I wanted to surprise you." His eyes filled with tears. "Please say you will. Please, Naomi. Say you'll marry me."

She blinked rapidly and let his words settle into her brain, into her heart. Her mouth dropped open. "You want to *marry me?*" she uttered.

"I love you." He stood stiffly, as if afraid she would disappear. "I have for a long time now."

"Zach!"

He grinned at her, and it was as if all the world's light broke forth on his face. "Quit saying my name."

She laughed then, a joyous sound enveloping both of them. "Never," she teased. "I will *never* stop saying your name. *Zach.*" Naomi's voice had gone breathless. "I love you, too."

He put his arms around her and lifted her from the cart, setting her feet gently on the grass. She lay against him, snuggling her head beneath his chin. He kissed the top of her *kapp* and let out a sigh of obvious relief.

But Naomi couldn't stay still. She pulled away. "But all this time, *all this time*, I didn't think you cared about me at all. You never said a thing."

Zach cast his eyes to the ground and went quiet. Then he looked at her. "I didn't think you cared about me. You were still reeling from Isaac's death." His eyes misted over. "And then, just as I thought you were healing, Justin Moore came into the picture."

Naomi flushed at his reference to the handsome *Englischer*. "I'm sorry. I was a fool. Like you said, I was still reeling, and I was hurting. I wasn't thinking straight."

He took both of her shoulders in his firm grasp. "I know you were hurting. And I was, well, I didn't handle Justin's appearance at the Bed and Breakfast well."

"If I'd known how you felt..."

He shook his head. "*Nee*, Naomi. It wouldn't have made a difference."

She looked into his eyes, and she'd never been so certain of anything in her life. "But it would have. I wouldn't have accepted Justin's sign, nor would I have welcomed him to stay again at the Bed and Breakfast. It would have made a great deal of difference. A great deal."

He gave a slight intake of breath and bent down to kiss her again. Raising his mouth from hers, he gazed deeply into her eyes. "So is that a yes? You'll marry me?"

She nodded as the tears coursed down her cheeks. "I'll marry you. Of course, I'll marry you!"

He grinned, and for a split second, she thought he would burst into tears, too. Then he asked, "Shall we tell the children?"

"Right away." She could hardly contain her excitement.

"Do you think they'll be all right with it?"

She smiled. "Ben will be over the moon. And Katy, ah, our dear Katy, she'll come around. And right quick, I'm thinking."

Zach squeezed her to him and then let her go. He tenderly helped her back into the pony cart, and she scooted over on the bench to make room for him. He climbed up and the cart dipped under his weight.

"Shall we go?"

Naomi nodded and looped her arm through his. "*Jah*," she said, and her voice was full of eager consent.

Epilogue

The ride back from Zach's house in the pony cart seems like a precious dream to me now. I think of that short trip often, remembering the joy that burst through me at every turn, and remembering how I glanced up at Zach constantly, feeling the need to reassure myself that he was really there, beside me.

I couldn't wait to get back to tell the children. And I couldn't wait to tell Mary. *I didn't have to leave!* I could stay in Hollybrook for the rest of my days.

Never, for an instant, did I think I would fall in love again after Isaac died. If I ever remarried, I figured it would be mostly for my children's sake. For them to have a father figure in their lives, and for all of us to have someone to help provide for us. I never thought I'd fall so deeply in love with another man.

But I did. I love Zach so much that sometimes it takes my breath away. I don't think of Zach in comparison to Isaac. I don't really even think of him as my second husband. There's no need. Isaac's and my life chapter together is complete. A cherished, much-loved memory. But Zach is my husband in his own way, and our love is unique in that it belongs to just the two of us. God has indeed blessed me far beyond what I ever dreamed possible.

When we got back to my farm that afternoon, Marvin was pacing the porch. He was angry, but when he saw Zach with me, his expression turned first to curiosity and then relief. I knew he thought Zach was coming to tell him that he'd purchase the farm. When Zach shared his real intent, Marvin collapsed in a rocker and stared at us. I couldn't help but giggle—seeing Marvin speechless for once in his life did my heart good.

I went upstairs to find Ben and when I told him the news, he flew down the steps and into Zach's arms. The two of them remained like that, pressed together tightly for the longest time. I stood by and wept to see it. I wept for Isaac and all that he was missing. But mostly, I wept with joyous contentment that Ben was being given the gift of a second father.

Katy reacted much as I thought she would. Hesitant at first. Grumpy about it, too, if the truth be told. But Zach's quiet presence at every dinner for the following week softened her. And when she saw that her uncle approved, that went in Zach's favor, too. And of course, Katy wouldn't have to leave her best friend which was a very nice thing for her.

Since the marriage, she's come fully around. She even bakes a pie every now and then for Zach. If any of us touches it, she playfully slaps our hands away and announces that it's for Zach's appetite only.

My family back in Pennsylvania was shocked at the news to say the least. But I ended up getting kind letters from most of them. Marvin's assessment of Zach's fine character helped. They were especially mollified when I told them we'd try to make a trip out east to visit them soon.

But we won't be going for a while. Zach and I are awaiting our first *boppli*. The little one is due come August. A busy time, to be sure, what with the harvesting and the canning to be done. But I have Mary to help me. And Katy. Together, we will do just fine.

As for King's Bed and Breakfast, it is humming along. I usually have guests once or maybe twice a week. Which is enough for now. It would be hard to handle more.

My life is full. Full and happy. *Ach*, sometimes it feels like it's overflowing! Which after the last two years is wonderful, indeed.

I probably should mention that the sign *King's Bed and Breakfast* looks right fine at the end of the drive. On more than one occasion, I've stood before it solely to admire its beauty. It does a good job of bringing in new guests, too.

The End

Continue Reading...

Thank you for reading **Naomi's Story. Are you wondering what to read next?** Why not read ***The Mother's Helper?***

Here's a sample for you:

Nancy Slagel cradled the baby in her arms. She felt the sting of tears pushing against her eyelids and held the child closer. Why couldn't this child be hers? She was twenty-one, plenty old enough.

If only Mark hadn't...

She shuddered. She couldn't let her mind wander down that road. She just *couldn't*. She was sick to death of tears.

But why had he done it? And with her own *sister?* Her father had tried to make excuses for Susan. "She's always been so tender-hearted," he told her. "When Mark was hurt, and you were gone ... well, it was a work of the Lord *Gott*."

Really? Having her beau stolen by her own sister had been *God's work?* Hardly. And it wasn't like Nancy would have been gone for good. She'd been away for one night visiting her grandmother. *One night!* It just couldn't have been so simple. Susan must have had designs on Mark from the start.

And Mark? To be able to deflect that easily?

It didn't bear thinking about.

Nancy cuddled the sleeping babe. If it didn't bear thinking about, then why did her mind continually go there? Why did she torture herself with thoughts of Mark's betrayal? She blinked hard, willing her tears not to fall. Nobody wanted to be around a cry-baby. Especially when that cry-baby was twenty-one years old. In truth, Nancy was beginning to detest herself for her continual weeping.

If only she could stop it...

"Nancy?" her cousin Irene tiptoed into the room. "He asleep?"

"*Jah*." Nancy kissed the fluffy hair on top of the baby's head. "Shall I put him down?"

"Go ahead. He should sleep for a while now."

Nancy moved gracefully to the crib and lowered the child to the mattress. Zeke stirred, but only for a second. Then he put his thumb in his mouth and sucked earnestly, his eyes still closed.

The two cousins tip-toed out of the room.

"You need to rest," Nancy said. "Go on, now. I'll start supper. Where's Debbie?"

Irene yawned and rolled her shoulders as if they were paining her. "She's downstairs playing with her blocks. I shouldn't leave her for more than a second or two."

Nancy put her hand on Irene's arm. "I'm going down. You get a nap in while you can."

"A nap? It just don't seem right when there's so much to do."

"Irene," Nancy scolded her, "that's the reason for a mother's helper. Now, let me earn my keep."

Irene smiled, stifling another yawn. "All right. But I won't sleep long."

"Sleep as long as you like." Nancy smiled and slipped out of the room. She hurried downstairs and went immediately to the front room to check on Debbie.

The two-year-old was rolling on the floor, her arms stretched wide. The blocks were strewn all over the rag rug.

Nancy squatted down next to her. "Come on, Debbie. Want to help me work on supper?"

"*Jab!*" Debbie said with a giggle. She got right up and toddled toward the kitchen. Nancy laughed and followed her.

That evening, Nancy used the left-over meatloaf to make thick sandwiches. She served them with coleslaw, a bowl of pickles, fruit salad, and gooey chocolate cookies. Irene's husband, Philip, smacked his lips when he was finished.

"Mighty fine supper, Irene."

"Weren't me that made it," Irene said. "I slept the day away like a regular heathen."

"Nonsense," Nancy said. "You nursed the baby while I finished up. It was nothing."

"Well, I won't argue about who's responsible. But, thank you, kindly," Philip said.

Debbie sat in her highchair, smooshing a pickle over the tray. She patted the resulting juice with glee, splashing Irene who sat next to her.

"*Ach*, Debbie!" Irene cried. "Stop that, now."

Nancy jumped up and circled the table with her cloth napkin. She mopped up the juice and took the pickle away. "I think you're full, Debbie. What do you say?"

205

Debbie grinned up at her.

"Let me *red* up the kitchen," Irene said.

"We'll do it together," Nancy replied, taking Debbie out of her highchair.

"*Ach*, Nancy, I forgot," Philip said, standing. He walked to the bureau at the side of the dining area and picked up an envelope. "You got a letter today."

Nancy took the envelope from his hand. She dreaded looking at the return address. She didn't want to hear from home—she'd rather pretend her home didn't even exist.

"From your sister, I believe," Philip said, confirming Nancy's suspicions.

Susan again? Nancy had already received two letters from Susan, begging her for forgiveness, but Nancy wasn't having much success with that, God help her.

She glanced down and was surprised to see that the letter wasn't from Susan. It was from her younger sister, Linda. Relief swooshed through her. "Thank you, Philip," she murmured.

"Go on then, and read it," Irene said. "I'll start the clean-up. I'm sure you're eager to hear any news from home."

Nancy's gaze flew to her cousin. Irene met her eyes, and her face took on a sheepish look as if she'd just remembered why Nancy would *not* be eager to hear news from home—as if she'd just remembered why Nancy had been so anxious to leave home and become a mother's helper in the first place.

"Or read it later," Irene added lamely. She held Debbie in one arm, and the platter of cookies in the other. "Whatever you wish."

Irene ducked into the kitchen, leaving Nancy standing there, holding the letter. Philip had already gone into the front room. Nancy released her breath in a long sigh. She might as well get it over with. With any luck, Linda wouldn't mention either Susan or Mark.

The late April weather was unseasonably warm for central Indiana, so Nancy pushed through the screen door and went out to the front porch. She sat down on the porch swing and reluctantly opened the envelope. It was a thin letter, only one sheet of stationery.

Bracing herself, Nancy began to read.

Dear Nancy,

We're missing you here in Linnow Creek. Lots of people asked after you at the last youth singing. Mostly, though, the house seems empty without you. Mamm and Dat are fine. Although, Dat coughs a lot. He assures me that it's nothing, but sometimes in the night, I hear him.

Amos and Peter are fine, too. But brothers are never gut company like sisters are. I think of everyone here, I miss you the most.

Are you having warm weather in Hollybrook? We're not that far away, so I imagine our weather is about the same. I've already been leaving my window open at night. The bed seems mighty empty without you in it with me. Did you know that you can stretch wide and just barely touch the edges of the mattress?

Nancy paused and smiled. Leave it to Linda to make something silly out of having a bed to herself. Nancy hadn't minded sharing a room or a bed with Linda. They used to whisper long into the night about everything and nothing. It was a comfort to have such a close sister. Nancy's chest constricted. Truth be told, she missed Linda. But avoiding her home unfortunately meant avoiding Linda, too.

How is Cousin Irene? And little Debbie? And Zeke? Oh, he must be so precious. I'm envious of you in a way. I would love to be caring for a boppli. Maybe I can be a mother's helper someday for—

And here Linda had written something that she'd erased. Nancy swallowed. Had she written Susan's name and then smudged it out? Had she? Did this mean that Susan was engaged? Nancy sucked in her breath. No. That couldn't be. It wasn't yet the season to be published. But was she secretly engaged, and she'd let Linda in on the secret. Nancy dropped the letter in her lap and stared out over the front yard. The willow tree spreading above the freshly-cut grass was already fully leafed-out, and the clumps of daffodils below were in full bloom. It made a pretty picture: serene, colorful, full of new life. But Nancy didn't revel in the beauty as she usually would. Her mind was churning.

She forced herself to keep reading.

...Irene when she has her next boppli. Or you...

Ach, I'm sorry, Nancy. I shouldn't be talking about bopplis and such. I know your heart is still hurting. I'm so sorry. I should be with you. I miss you so much. You know I love Susan, too, but it's not the same. She never was that close to us, was she? I've often wondered about it.

She's hurting, too, Nancy. I think she's right sorry for how things turned out. I hope you can find it in your heart to forgive her. And then, our family can be whole again.

Mamm is sometimes weepy...

Nancy stopped reading. Susan ... sorry? Nancy didn't think so. If she was so sorry, she'd break it off with Mark, wouldn't she? If she was so sorry, she'd show it with her actions. Nancy licked her lips. Besides, she wasn't even there in Linnow Creek anymore, so her relationship with Susan shouldn't be a topic of concern.

She was now in Hollybrook, doing God's work, helping her cousin. No one could fault her for that, could they? And Nancy could hardly be blamed for breaking up her family. That was just Linda's sense of the dramatic.

In truth, Nancy's leaving had helped her family. She'd removed herself from a horrible situation. By exiting herself, she'd taken away the source of tension and conflict.

Nancy looked down at the letter again. She'd finish it later. She simply didn't have the heart to finish it right then. Nor did she have the heart to write back. She opened the screen door and went back inside.

"Irene?" she called. "Is Zeke ready to be put to bed?"

Irene popped her head out from the kitchen. "I'm going to nurse him in a minute, and I'll put him down. If you could get Debbie ready for bed, that would be wonderful."

"Of course. Glad to," Nancy said. She heard Debbie in the front room squealing about something. Then she heard Philip's deep laughter, and her heart caught.

She wanted a family of her own. A husband of her own. A child of her own.

Putting on a cheery smile, she entered the front room and swooped Debbie up into her arms.

To find this book, visit: http://brendamaxfield.com

Thank you for Reading

If you **love Amish Romance**, visit:

http://brendamaxfield.com/newreleasenotice.html

to find out about all **New Hollybrook Amish Romance Releases! We will let you know as soon as they become available!**

If you enjoyed *Naomi's Story* would you kindly take a couple minutes to leave a positive review on Amazon? It only takes a moment, and it truly makes a difference. I would be so grateful! Thank you!

Turn the page to discover more Amish Romances just for you!

More Hollybrook Amish Romances
for You

Hollybrook Love!

**Amish Romance Bonanza! 11 Amish Romances, sweet, clean &
inspirational! GET ALL ELEVEN Romances for ONE
GREAT PRICE!!**

Finding Home!

Get 6 COMPLETE romances in one volume **and at a great bargain
price!**

Nancy's Story #1: The Mother's Helper

**Betrayed, Nancy Slagel flees to Hollybrook to become a
mother's helper. However, she doesn't count on meeting Luke
Rupp. She notices his good looks and charming demeanor, but**

he is restless and rebellious, and more than a little disturbing. Nancy came looking for peace and healing, but what she finds is so much more…

Nancy's Story #2: Losing Ariel

Nancy Slagel dreads her growing feelings for Luke Rupp. She secretly hopes for romance but discovers that Luke's previous *Englisch* girlfriend has returned. Tragedy strikes, and Luke flees back to the *Englisch* world. Nancy wonders whether she'll ever see him again. She does, but he's different. Marked. Nancy has no idea whether he'll ever recover or ever truly see her in the same light again.

Greta's Story #1: Replacement Wife

Isaac Wagner gapes at his dying wife. Does she really expect him to marry Greta Glick after she dies? How can anyone replace Betty as his wife? How can anyone replace her as the mother to their son? Isaac can't even begin to think such thoughts. All he wants is for his wife to live. But Isaac's prayers aren't answered.

Greta's Story #2: The Promise

Greta and Isaac promise Isaac's wife that they will marry each other upon her death. But when Betty dies, Isaac leaves the state. Greta is left in turmoil, harboring her secret love for Isaac. Having no choice, Greta moves on with her life and meets Todd Fisher. He brings laughter to her life and life holds promise again. Isaac returns, now, what will happen? Will Isaac expect her to carry out the promise? Or will he set them both free?

Greta's Story #3: The Wedding

Greta gapes at her fiancé. Isaac doesn't want an Amish wedding? Greta can't help but wonder whether she's doing the right thing to marry him. Todd Fisher watches closely as the wedding arrangements go forward. He knows the real reason behind Greta's engagement, and he doesn't approve. He loves her--does Isaac? Todd isn't about to stand by and let the wedding happen without trying again.

Rhoda's Story #1: The Amish Beekeeper!

People consider Rhoda Hilty an established spinster, which never bothered her—until Aaron Raber comes to town. When he approaches her to rent her beehives for his struggling orchard, Rhoda's world turns upside down. But how can she be interested in him when she's so busy caring for her aging senile mother? Besides ... Aaron's interest in her is strictly business. Isn't it?

Rhoda's Story #2: The Accident!

Rhoda Hilty struggles to keep her promise to her elderly mother. But when a tragic accident occurs, Rhoda is forced to break her promise. In addition, Rhoda has to care for her sister's family as well as her mother. When will it be Rhoda's turn? How will her handsome neighbor Aaron Raber ever see her as more than a spinster daughter and sister?

Rhoda's Story #3: Coming Home!

Rhoda Hilty's heart cries out as she watches her mother refuse food. Winnie is wasting away, and Rhoda feels helpless. And now Rhoda's sweetheart, Aaron Raber, is gone. Writing letters to him is better than nothing, but Rhoda yearns for him. Aaron has promised that when he returns, they will court. But will he ever be free to come back to Hollybrook? It doesn't appear so.

Faith's Story #1: The Adoption!

Faith Baldwin's birth mother is Amish and lives somewhere in Indiana, and she's determined to find her. Pretending she's a tourist, she digs around for clues. While there, she becomes enchanted with the Amish and their way of life. But things don't go as smoothly as she hopes. Her boyfriend unexpectedly shows up; every lead goes dead; and the one old woman who might have answers for her won't talk.

Faith's Story #2: Changing Her Mind! Her birth mother had written. With trembling hands, Faith Baldwin rips open the flap. Her eyes fly over the words until she finds the closing. *Your mother, Nancy...* Faith and her birth mother begin a correspondence that brings them both blissful joy. However, Nancy's husband discovers her secret child, and his anger and sense of betrayal build an insurmountable wall between them. And if the truth is made public, how could Nancy explain a grown daughter to her children or her community?

Faith's Story #3: Home at Last!

Faith Baldwin has her wish. She is sitting face-to-face with her Amish birth mother. As Faith struggles to fit in with her new Amish family, the hole in her heart begins to heal. But she yearns to truly belong, to truly *be* Amish. But that would mean closing down everything about her former life. It would mean starting over.

Mellie's Story #1: Mellie's Sweet Shop!

Mellie Fisher is in love with her sister's beau. Striving to keep it a secret, she suffers in silence. When her sister makes a rash decision, Mellie prays that her chance with the handsome, kind Caleb Glick has finally come. But with her brother's family moving into their already crowded house, and her mother's illness creating chaos, Mellie worries that she will never have her chance at love. Will she forever be known as the single Amish girl who bakes sweets? Or is there something more for her?

Mellie's Story #2: Leaving Hollybrook!

Beth Fisher spurns her steady beau to follow her dream of teaching. Leaving her family, she travels to Meadow Lark to become their new teacher. When school begins, it's as wonderful as she expected. What she doesn't expect, however, is to meet Timothy Plank, a widower with three children. She refuses to hear her heart where Timothy is concerned, and she rejects his love for her. But is teaching truly enough to fulfill her forever? Is she willing to give it up to find love?

Mellie's Story #3: The Fire!

Mellie Fisher is weary of pining over her sister's former beau. How long must she wait for his affection? Despairing, she agrees to be courted by Obadiah Westman. But things don't go as planned, and she quickly regrets her decision. Her mother's catastrophic fall, a disaster at her Sweet Shop, and her sister-in-law's accident all conspire to derail Mellie's happiness and plans for the future. How can it ever be good again? And will she ever gain Caleb's love?

Naomi's Story #1: Byler's Bed and Breakfast!

Still reeling from her husband's death, Naomi Byler struggles to support herself and her two children. A chance meeting with a handsome *Englischer* gives her the opportunity to open a Bed and Breakfast. Naomi meets resistance from Zachariah King, the young Amish farmer who leases her land. Is Zachariah *interested* in her? And if he is, why doesn't he *say* anything? And is the handsome *Englischer* wanting more than room and board? *Are the two men now in competition?*

Naomi's Story #2: The Englischer Stayed Twice!

The widow Naomi Byler struggles to forget the handsome *Englischer* who stayed at her Bed and Breakfast. With time, his effect on her fades, and life resumes. Naomi's relationship with Zach King grows as Naomi's grief over her husband's death heals. But when the *Englischer* suddenly returns with a gift, disruption reigns. Naomi is thrown into a tailspin, and Zach is at first angry then grows distant. Is Naomi about to lose her hard-won peace? Is she about to enter a place where there's no hope of forgiveness?

Naomi's Story #3: Naomi's Choice!

BRENDA MAXFIELD

The Englischer is gone. While Naomi mourns his leaving, she hopes that Zach King will now declare his feelings for her. But Zach remains painfully quiet. When Naomi's brother comes to Hollybrook and insists that she and her children move back to Pennsylvania, she panics. Not wanting to leave her Bed and Breakfast, her friends, or Zach, she makes one final last-ditch effort. But will it have any effect at all? Or will she have to leave everything she's worked so hard to build?

Annie's Story #1: The Forbidden Baby!

Not wanting to burden others, Annie Braus works to maintain a pleasant attitude. But lurking beneath, she harbors deep sorrow. Wondering if things will ever change, she fights against feelings of anger toward God. When her sister dives off the deep end during *rumspringa* and ends up in serious trouble, Annie wonders whether this might be God's answer for her. But how can her sister's mistake become Annie's blessing? And will Annie's husband go along with her father's daring plan?

Annie's Story #2: Escaping Acre's Corner!

Refusing to give in to her father's plan, Sarah Clapper plots her escape carefully. Her *Englisch* boyfriend joins her, whisking her away from her cousin's Amish home. Sarah thought marriage would solve her problem, but it only makes things worse. She is stunned to find herself yearning for home. Her Amish home. But certain things in life that cannot be reversed. Has Sarah trapped herself? Is there any way for her to get out of the mess she's made?

Annie's Story #3: Sarah's Return!

Annie Braus goes numb with relief when her pregnant runaway sister returns. But when Sarah reveals that she secretly married an Englisch boy, Annie fears the worst.

Now how can she and Amos claim Sarah's baby as their own? And if Sarah is married, where is her husband? Annie

216

struggles to take care of her sister, through a harrowing late-night scare, an unwelcome visitor, and a shocking revelation of her own.

Josie's Story #1: The Schoolteacher's Baby

All John Beiler wants is to escape his grief. He bundles up his baby daughter and flees to Hollybrook. With a numb heart, he engages Josie Bontrager to care for his baby. When he starts to fall for Josie, he resists. How can he risk loving again? And wouldn't it dishonor his deceased wife to have feelings for another?

Josie's Story #2: A Desperate Act!

Secret meetings behind closed doors. Furtive looks. Strange, unexplained behavior. What is John Beiler involved in? Josie is desperate to find out, but her beau remains stubbornly silent. Does it have anything to do with Amanda Crabill and her son?

Sally's Story #1: The Decision

For Sally, leaving the Amish would mean leaving Zeke. Can she ignore her feelings for him and turn her back on her dreams? And all for a brother who doesn't want her around?

Sally's Story #2: Second Thoughts

"It wouldn't work. It couldn't work. We are from two different worlds, you and me." Zeke gazed at her, his eyes filled with infinite sadness.

Sally won't give up. But will she burn all the bridges she's worked so hard to build?

Sally's Story #3: The Stranger

Who is this stranger? And does he have the legal right to take her away as he claims? How can Sally convince the stranger to let her go? And how will she ever get back to Zeke?

Amish Days 1: Missing Abram

Are Hope's dreams of Abram only a fantasy? Will his cousin Josiah try to step in?

Amish Days 2: Abram's Plan

Mysterious relatives force Hope to leave her Amish home. While gone, her fiancé Abram is hurt. Will he heal? Can she ever go back?

Amish Days 3: Abram's Bride

Why is Abram refusing to marry Hope? Hadn't he promised her a November wedding? Was she to be a jilted bride?

Amish Days: The Runaway!

Caught in a cocoon of cold and desperation, will Mary admit her feelings for Josiah? Will Josiah confirm Mary's suspicions that it's really her sister that he loves?

Amish Days: A Loving Stranger

After a full year of professing his love, Ezra Ebersol dumps Sadie and becomes engaged to another girl. Sadie reels with her pain and confusion for weeks. Hiding out, she encounters a stranger. She tries to evade him, but newcomer Joshua Graber isn't so easily dissuaded. When Sadie discovers the reason for her broken relationship with Ezra, her eyes are opened. Was Joshua sent to help her heal? Or is he just another person who can't be trusted?

Marian's Story #1: The Amish Blogger

Marian Yoder befriends an *Englisch* girl—never dreaming it will lead her to a blog of her own. Nor that it would catch the eye of the handsome *Englisch* guy, Roger Young. Marian gets sucked into their exciting world. But her mother's frightening behavior brings turmoil and danger. When Thomas Groft turns his eye toward Marian, she's caught in the middle.

Marian's Story #2: Missing Mama

Marian Yoder can't wait to marry Thomas Groft. But when

her mother is admitted to a sanitarium, Marian is forced to become caretaker to her baby sister. Marian can't leave her father or baby sister to marry Thomas. When she learns her mother has run away, her faith is tested to the near breaking point. Will there ever be a way for Marian to marry Thomas?

Marian's Story #3: The Big Freeze

Marian marries her sweetheart and dreams of a loving future. But reality steps in to destroy her vision. Her mother-in-law's resentment threatens to poison the very love Marian holds for her new husband. When Marian discovers the shocking reason behind her mother-in-law's nasty treatment, she's horrified. Tragedy strikes, and the whole family is plunged into fear and turmoil. Marian has the chance to save the day, but will it do any good?

www.brendamaxfield.com

About the Author

My passion is writing! What could be more delicious than inventing new characters and seeing where they take you?

I am blessed to live in Indiana, a state I share with many Amish communities. (I find the best spices, hot cereal, and good cooking advice at an Amish store not too far away.)

I've lived in Honduras, Grand Cayman, and Costa Rica. One of my favorite activities is exploring other cultures. My husband, Paul, and I have two grown children and four precious grandchildren, three, special delivery from Africa and one, homegrown. I love to hole up in our lake cabin and write -- often with a batch of popcorn nearby. (Oh, and did I mention dark chocolate?)

I enjoy getting to know my readers, so feel free to write me at: contact@brendamaxfield.com. Join my Newsletter Gang and get the latest news about releases: brendamaxfield.com/newreleasenotice.html. Visit me to learn about all my books: brendamaxfield.com Happy Reading!

www.brendamaxfield.com
contact@brendamaxfield

Made in United States
Orlando, FL
18 April 2024

45940025R00124